THE KAFKA EFFEKT
D. Harlan Wilson

ERASERHEAD PRESS

THE ERASERHEAD COLLECTIVE

Acknowledgement is made to the following publications in which these stories first appeared:

"Boyeraqueri Bubbolifiticus's Body": *Lethogica*, 2000. "Inside the Tin Man": *Redsine* (Australia), 2000. "Beneath the Husband": *The Nocturnal Lyric*, 2000. "Feet": *Driver's Side Airbag*, 2001. "Room": *Redsine* (Australia), 2001. "The Walls": *Doorknobs & BodyPaint*, 1999. "Circus": *The Café Irreal*, 2000. "The Cocktail Party": *Redsine* (Australia), 2001. "At the Funeral": *Samsara Quarterly*, 2001. "The Stranger in the Manhole": *Driver's Side Airbag*, 2000. "The Eagle-Headed Man in the Airport": *The Dream Zone* (UK), 2001. "Conversation with a Hair Stylist": *Doorknobs & BodyPaint*, 1999. "The Wiener Dog on the Ceiling": *The Dream People*, 2000. "My Mother's Pillows": *Redsine* (Australia), 2000. "Look'd Too Near": *Driver's Side Airbag*, 2000. "The Cape": *The Café Irreal*, 2001. "A Concern": *Redsine* (Australia), 2000.

"Schoolgirl Road Rage," "The Nose," "Punch Line," "The Mouths," "The Truth About Humpty Dumpty," and "In Supercalifragilistic City" all appeared in the chapbook *Kafka-Breathing Sock Puppets*, published by Eraserhead Press in 2000.

ISBN 0-9713572-1-8

Eraserhead Press
16455 E. Fairlynn Dr,
Fountain Hills, AZ 85268
email: ehpress@aol.com
website: www.eraserheadpress.com

For my sister Jain

"It is midnight, but since I have slept very well, that is an excuse only to the extent that by day I would have written nothing. The burning electric light, the silent house, the darkness outside, the last waking moments, they give me the right to write even if it be only the most miserable stuff. And this right I use hurriedly. That's the person I am."

— Franz Kafka, 24 December 1910 entry in *Diaries*

"Even when it is unique, a language remains a mixture, a schizophrenic mélange, a Harlequin costume in which very different functions of language and distinct centers of power are played out, blurring what can be said and what can't be said."

— Deleuze and Guattari, *Kafka: Towards a Minor Literature*

CONTENTS

WARNING ON A PERSON

WARNING: This person contains a hairtrigger temper and should be handled with care. Do not unnerve by means of dirty looks, shallow-mindedness, body odor, brown teeth, mullet hairdos, social ineptitude, pathological oneupmanship, use of the word *pejorative* under any circumstance, pec flexing, or attachment of extremities to jumper cables. **FLAMMABLE:** Not to be held over a forest fire. **FRAGILE:** Not to be wrapped in duct tape and beaten to death with a knee sock full of British pounds. Not for use as a watercraft. Avoid excessive exposure to sunlight, nuclear waste, political machines, solitude, reruns of The Lawrence Welk Show, and postmodern novels over 500 pages long. Do not spit on. Do not sniff or lick and if you do sniff or lick, do not wince at and complain about the smell or taste. Treat with extreme suspicion and do not trust. At the same time, do not hate: this person will know if you hate him. Keep out of reach of children, pregnant women, manic depressives, octogenarians, strippers, conspiracy theorists, hillbillies, schizophrenics, liquor stores, tax collectors, capitalists, marxists, movie stars, and persons that have warnings like this one tattooed onto their forehead. The maximum recommended dosage of this person for a healthy adult is fifteen seconds; if this dosage is exceeded, consult your local witch doctor. Use as directed. (**NOTE:** Improper use of this person may result in the Apocalypse according to John.)

BOYERAQUERI BUBBOLIFITICUS'S BODY

Boyeraqueri Bubbolifiticus is very ugly-looking in that rather than hair growing out of his skin he has hair-sized clones of Marlon Brando, except on his head and face, which is shaggy with clones of Michael Wincott, an underrated actor with a smoke-scraped voice who almost invariably plays a villain. There is also his ugly name, Boyeraqueri Bubbolifiticus, which sounds more like a disease than a man's name; but whenever he introduces himself he usually just says, "I'm Bob," and leaves it at that, not knowing how to pronounce Boyeraqueri Bubbolifiticus anyway.

Boyeraqueri Bubbolifiticus is not a particularly insecure or vain man and he does not actively seek out the acclaim of his peers. Still, he would much rather have hair on his body instead of little Marlon Brandos and Michael Wincotts, if only to get a little peace and quiet. But if he could have it any way, he would have nothing at all, not a hair or actor or anything on his body, he would be smooth, smooth, smooth! All he had to do was shave his body from head to toe. And he would shave his body from head to toe. He shaved it every morning, early, while the Brandos and Wincotts were still asleep.

Outside Boyeraqueri Bubbolifiticus's window an elephant pigeon tread air and shat.

Inside Boyeraqueri Bubbolifiticus's window Boyeraqueri Bubbolifiticus undressed and removed shaving cream and a Gillette SensorExcel razor from a bathroom drawer. He stepped into a large bathtub and delicately, very delicately, so very delicately that not even the lightest of his sleepers would wake, wet himself down with a warm washcloth, then applied a light film of shaving cream to his legs, genitals, ass, stomach, chest, forearms, armpits, neck, face, eyebrows and head. Then he began shaving.

As the first stripe of Marlon Brandos was removed from his lower left calf everybody was jarred awake by the shaved off Brandos' squeak-screams of agony. "Stella!" carped a patch of groggy Brandos located on the back of Boyeraqueri Bubbolifiticus's hand, the one holding the razor, and this sparked a wave of protests and complaints, from Brandos and Wincotts alike (albeit the Wincotts were less aggressive than the Brandos), to ripple back and forth across Boyeraqueri Bubbolifiticus's body.

Unfazed, Boyeraqueri Bubbolifiticus kept on shaving, cutting off a hundred Marlon Brandos at the kneecaps with each swipe of his razor and then washing the razor off beneath the bathroom faucet. "The horror, the horror!" the Brandos gurgled as, spurting and gesticulating, they were scalded by a gush of hot water that pushed them into the bathtub drain. The Wincotts, in contrast, arbitrarily gurgled lines from *Strange Days*, *The Crow*, *1492: Conquest of Paradise*, *Dead Man* and *Along Came a Spider*, all films in which the real Michael Wincott appears.

It took Boyeraqueri Bubbolifiticus an hour to shave himself in his entirety. When he was finished, he washed what corpses remained out of the bathtub and then sat down in the bathtub, and closed his eyes. Every single one of his pores was bleeding and he had to wait for the bleeding to stop. It took another hour. During that hour Boyeraqueri Bubbolifiticus had a dream about a dish rag. The dish rag had marinated itself in a special substance and when it jumped on his face it wiped the face off. All that was left on Boyeraqueri Bubbolifiticus's head was a ruff of hair and two ears and a smooth patch of skin where his facial features used to be. He wanted to tell the dish rag to give him back his face, but he didn't have a mouth. This made him want to sniffle and cry, but he had no nose and no eyes or tear ducts either. He had some ears, though, and so he waited for the dish rag to say something to him; hopefully it would explain why it had jumped on and stolen his face. Then he remembered that dish rags don't have mouths and he did the only thing he could do: curl up in a ball and roll away . . .

His entire body winedark and a bit crusty in places, Boyeraqueri Bubbolifiticus opened his eyes. He stood and turned the shower on, and showered. When he was finished he dried off and took two tetracycline capsules and with a washcloth nursed the spots on his body that were still bleeding. There were many spots, but eventually the blood stopped flowing . . . and a permagrin ravaged Boyeraqueri Bubbolifiticus's face.

"I'm Bob," permagrinned Boyeraqueri Bubbolifiticus as he inspected his smooth, smooth, smooth body in the mirror. He was very happy. But how long would he remain very happy? Not very long. No more than forty-five minutes. So Boyeraqueri Bubbolifiticus, intent on enjoying and savoring his happiness while it lasted, began prancing back and forth in front of his window, and sometimes he would pause and do breakdance moves, or do impersonations of politicians, or pick his pets up— he had a beaver, an algae-eater and a two piglets—by the tails and swing them overhead like lassos, or just flex his muscles. There was no longer an elephant pigeon treading air and shitting outside his window, but there were a bunch of people, about thirty or so, all tied to balloons by strings wrapped around their ears, all straight-faced and blinking at the little performance.

Forty-four minutes later Boyeraqueri Bubbolifiticus sensed his smooth-bodied glee coming to an end. Sighing, he turned away from his window and went over to his couch and sat down and turned on his tv, and waited for it to happen.

This is what happened: Thousands and thousands of infinitesimal Marlon Brando and Michael Wincott heads started poking up out of Boyeraqueri Bubbolifiticus's skin, making him all itchy, but he didn't itch, itching would only make it worse, so he continued to watch tv, there was a Bewitched marathon on and he was in love with Elizabeth Montgomery, and as he sat there loving Elizabeth Montgomery, the Marlon Brando mouths on his body and the Michael Wincott mouths on his face and head were exposed, and these mouths attacked Boyeraqueri Bubbolifiticus with the foulest language, rendering him nothing less than a loudspeaker of obscenity, and he had to blast the volume on the tv in order to hear Elizabeth Montgomery make her jokes, but he couldn't hear her jokes, his body and head were too loud, so he had to settle for just watching Elizabeth Montgomery smile and move her lips while listening to the abuse that was raining down upon him from within him, difficult to make out since so many mouths were squeak-screaming at once, but he could make out the odd "Sonuvabitch asshole killer!" and before Boyeraqueri Bubbolifiticus knew it the torsos of the Brandos and Wincotts were up, torsos that flailed and shook their arms and fists, beating against Boyeraqueri Bubbolifiticus's flesh as hard as they possibly could so that in a very short time period he was not only a loudspeaker of obscenity but a giant bruise too, and bruises pulse with pain, pulse, pulse, pulse with pain, and Boyeraqueri Bubbolifiticus was no longer very happy, he was very very unhappy, especially when the Brandos and Wincotts were fully grown again, up to their knees in his skin, and in addition to beating on and swearing at him they started quoting lines from Shakespeare and driving their landlord, as it were, who had overdosed on Shakespeare as a young man and couldn't even stand to hear the name Shakespeare uttered, to the edge of insanity, and then over the edge, straight into the pit of psychosis, at the bottom of which Elizabeth Montgomery was getting gang-fondled by a slavering wolfpack of genies and liking it, and a horrified, breathless, pain-charged Boyeraqueri

Bubbolifiticus passed out, free fell into a cold hard sleep that terminated in morning, early in the morning, when Boyeraqueri Bubbolifiticus's body was still asleep.

INSIDE THE TIN MAN

My girlfriend walked over to the window sill and picked up the tin man. She picks things up all the time, and I hate her for it. You should see her in a furniture store. It's so embarrassing.

"Why do you always have to pick things up?" I asked her.

She ignored me. Or maybe I didn't speak loud enough and she just didn't hear what I said. But even if she didn't hear what I said, she had to hear me say something, I don't care if I was whispering, which I wasn't, and so her not acknowledging me, not even looking over her shoulder and saying "Huh?" led me to believe that she was definitely ignoring me.

I was about to tell my girlfriend I hated her when she asked, "What's in this?" as she turned the tin man over in her hands. The tin man was no bigger than a beer bottle and had a label pasted onto its forehead that read: FRAGILE!!! I worried that she would break him, if not with her nosy little fingers, then by dropping him on the floor.

With urgency in my voice I ordered my girlfriend to carefully put the tin man back where he belonged.

Now she looked over her shoulder at me. Clearing her throat, she said, "Why won't you tell me what's inside of him?"

I bit my tongue. I bit my tongue until I could taste blood. "How am I supposed to know what's inside of him?" I exclaimed. "How am I supposed to know that? It could be anything. Anything! Popcorn kernels. Nuts and bolts. Dead cockroaches. Human toes. Toxic waste. Fiberoptics. Dirt. A black hole. You name it. What do I know about what's inside that tin man? I've never even seen him before in my life. Maybe there's organs inside of him, organs like yours and mine. Maybe there's nothing. Have you ever considered that there might be nothing inside of him? And even if there's *something* inside of him, does it really matter? No, it doesn't. So will you put him down now? You're making me uncomfortable. As always."

After turning the tin man over a few more times in her hands, and then lifting him next to her ear and shaking him— no rattling noise—my girlfriend reluctantly did what I told her. Then she left, without a word, obviously angry at me. I didn't care. Not at that moment at least. I'd make her feel better later. Or maybe I wouldn't make her feel better, maybe I'd just break up with her. I had been wanting to for a long time and if I was man enough, I'd do it. Was I man enough? Man enough to cut that baggage loose?

But I couldn't think about my stupid girlfriend right now. Right now, there was something I wanted to do.

I walked over to the window sill, kneeled down and looked into the tin man's jeweled eyes. I was about to touch his right eye with the tip of my pinky finger when his little mouth smiled at me and chirped, "Thank you very much, sir."

I was a bit surprised at first. I hadn't expected the tin man to be so polite and I think I might have even gasped. But I quickly pulled myself together and, so as not to be rude, replied, "You're very welcome."

For a while the tin man and I just stared at each other. He had really beautiful eyes.

Then I glanced over both of my shoulders, to see if anybody was watching me, and finally I picked him up and ripped off his head and looked down his open neck, to see what I could see.

A DESCRIPTION

The girl with the seaweed hair is pacing back and forth across the desert and words are falling out of her mouth like beach-weathered pieces of glass. She doesn't know that she's about to be shot through the forehead with a petrified lobster eyeball, nor does she know that the eyeball will be fired at her with a souped-up belly button that is not only a belly button, it's an asshole and a gun, too. But what she doesn't know is not important. What is important is that the petrified lobster eyeball is doomed to strike the talking, pacing girl and soon doom is right on top of her. Her neck cracks back and blood spits out of her forehead in bursting bubbles. She crumbles to her knees. Words continue to fall from her mouth (although now they fall like dank pine cones) as her ostrich head falls into the white sand and takes root and her body stiffens into a fire hydrant splattered with shark piss and pterodactyl shit. A few minutes of silence and inertia pass before her water valve unexpectedly comes loose. A few minutes of screaming and pandemonium pass as a lattice of buildings, stairways, catwalks, ladders, manholes and mannequins leaks out of the water valve and surrounds her, and stares at her.

BENEATH THE HUSBAND

The husband sits on the back porch of a house on a hill. After the sun goes down, he goes inside and sits on a couch. A cold fireplace is in front of him. He watches it. There are no flames. But he pretends there are of thousands of them. Thousands of living, breathing flames.

An hour passes. The husband begins to doze off. He dozes off and on for hours.

He happens to be on when the wife skulks by the fireplace.

She has snow white skin on her body and long blonde hair on her head. She's naked and the hair between her legs is also long and blonde—and wound into a thick swinging braid. As she skulks her arms wave about in front of her, dumbly, of their own boneless volition.

Suddenly her arms fall down. "Ta da," says the wife and takes a bow.

"Ta da *what*," replies the husband. He winces and squirms uncomfortably. Then he points at the wife's vagina. "What have you done with your hair? More importantly, *why* have you done it?"

The wife straightens up. She looks at the husband and makes a face. She makes two more faces, each of them as different from one another as from the first face she made. The fourth face she makes is not a face at all in that her face is so expressionless it ceases to be a face.

"I've got something to show you," she says without moving her lips. The husband knows she wants him to ask her why she doesn't move her lips. But he doesn't. He shrugs, wishing the wife would get out of the way. She's blocking his view of the fireplace and now he has to lean his head over and peek around her hips if he wants to get a look at the flames. To hear the flames hum and crackle is not enough; they must be seen, too.

The husband is about to tell the wife to get rid of herself when the wife lifts up a spread-fingered hand and places it on the lower half of her face. "Grrr," she says in a tone that is both playful and vicious. Then, with her fingers, she crawls up her nose and pinches the fold of skin between her eyes. Pinches that fold of skin, and pulls—

With a sucking noise the body suit comes off. The wife holds it out in front of her for a moment, then lets it drop to the floor. It splats against it like twelve pounds of tripe. The wife grins. She bows again, straightens up again.

Standing before the husband is a fully clothed woman with short-cropped black hair. Her skin is olive-toned. She's wearing a neatly pressed business suit and pantyhose with runs in them. She has the physiognomy of the husband's wife and seems to have her physique . . . but is she the husband's wife? He thinks so. He's certain of it, in fact. Still, his jaw falls into his lap. Gripping the couch pillow beneath him for support, he looks back and forth between his wife and the body suit until he grows dizzy and decides to take a nap.

When he wakes the husband says, "I don't think I understand."

Still grinning, the wife cocks her head. "Neither do I. But here I am. This is the *real* me. And look!" In three long strides the wife moves over to a closet. She opens it, rummages around inside of it, and removes the children. There are three of them, all under ten years old. One is the boy, one is the girl, one is the hermaphrodite. They are all wearing the same outfit: white sneakers, blue jeans, and red t-shirts with flashy generic insignias on the left breast. They are all emaciated. Their cheeks are flushed and crusted over with vomit and dried-up tears.

The wife lines the children up in front of the husband and begins to circle them. The children begin to sniffle and tremble. The husband can see the fireplace over their heads, save when the wife walks by him and temporarily mars his view. "What are you driving at?" he says impatiently. "Get to the point and get out." The wife's new look is making him feel more and more uneasy.

"I'm going, don't worry," she assures him, "but I want to show you something first. Okay? Can I show you something? It won't take long. It won't take more than a few seconds! Okay? Then I'll leave you alone. Alone with your fire. Okay?"

The husband stares at her. He scratches his crotch.

"Okay!" blurts the wife and without wasting any time she grabs hold of the son by the fold of skin between his eyes and as quickly as she removed her own body suit removes his and tosses it aside. She does the same to the daughter and the hermaphrodite. Stepping back, she presents the children to the husband with a sweeping motion of her arm and once again says, "Ta da!" She pauses before bowing, glaring at the children out of the corners of her eyes as if waiting for them to misbehave in some way.

Blinking and frowning, the husband examines the children. He doesn't get up off the couch but he does lean over and rest his elbows on his knees. And his neck stretches out towards the children as far as it possibly can.

Unlike the wife's new look, which more or less resembles her old look aside from the hair and clothes and skin color, the children's new looks don't look a thing like their old ones, even though their sizes remain the same.

What used to be the boy is now a stark, white skeleton.

It has chattering teeth and pulsing red eyes, and is a cartoon.

Beneath the girl is a little werewolf. It's cross-eyed. Entirely unthreatening, it drools all over itself and wags its bushy tail.

The hermaphrodite has become a hairy, prickly cactus, without limbs, standing in a pot of dirt. This upsets the husband the most. Why? It's not because he loved the hermaphrodite more than the boy or the girl. He loved them all just the same. So why does the hermaphrodite's changing into a cactus irk him so much? Is it because a cactus is less human, or less anthropomorphic anyway, than a werewolf or skeleton? Or is it because . . .

But wait a second, the husband says to himself. The children haven't changed into anything. They've always been this way. They've always been the skeleton, the werewolf and the cactus. Those things are the real. The boy, the girl, the hermaphrodite—those things were just the apparent.

Unless the wife is playing some kind of joke on me . . .

Before the husband has an opportunity to open his mouth and interrogate her, the wife has already gathered up the children, carried them back over to the closet and tossed them in there, and shut the door.

"Good night sweetheart," she says, picks up a briefcase and leaves. Unable to speak at this point, the husband watches her go. He thinks she will turn around and come back to him, and talk to him. She doesn't.

Sitting back in the couch and chewing on his tongue, he turns to the fireplace. The flames inside of it are still going strong. But he's unable to fully concentrate on them. In his periphery are the body suits, left all over the floor for him to clean up, by the wife. He's trying to relax here and he can't relax in a messy room. The wife knows this. The wife knows the husband knows the wife knows this, too, and so he curses her before talking himself into getting off the couch and picking up the body suits and tossing them into a trash can, one by one. Then he has to go get a mop and clean up the slimy residue left behind by the body suits, and finally he throws the head of the mop into the trash can, this after breaking the stick of the mop up into four pieces and trashing that.

Feeling winded, the husband goes to sit down on the couch again. He hesitates. He turns and faces the fireplace, and begins to massage his jaw.

Should I try it? he wonders. I'm afraid to. And with each passing second I'm becoming more and more afraid. If I don't try it now I never will. I have to act fast here if I'm going to act at all. Should I try it now? Is that what *she* wants me to do? If it is, I don't want to do it. If it isn't, I don't want to do it . . .

. . . The husband decides to do it.

Gripping his entire brow with all five of his fingers, he closes his eyes and gives himself a quick, ferocious yank. There is a sucking noise followed by a gasp. There is the sound of a body suit splatting against the floor. There is the husband opening his eyes and looking into the fireplace . . . and seeing nothing. No flames. Even when he pretends there are flames he sees no flames. In the fireplace is a wrought-iron grill with some old ashes beneath it, that's all. It's so disturbing that the husband completely forgets about himself—until, that is, he sits back down on the couch, and the couch, and the fireplace in front of it, and the house surrounding it, and the hill that the house sits on top of, and the world beneath the hill—until all these things catch fire, and go up in the flames of the real.

THE MAN AND I

We were face to face, eye to eye, breath to breath—and the fuzzy little hairs on the tips of our noses had synaptically fused together, so that the man's life force flowed into my own, making it my own, and vice versa. I admit I had been taken by surprise. We had only come together in the last few moments, after all, following what seemed like an interminable approach across the wasted, naked plane, he approaching from the horizon in the east, I from the one in the west. We moved rapidly at first—I seem to remember sprinting at top speed, my body no less than a sparkling grey blur; but so much time has passed since the beginning, to put faith in my memory would be as ludicrous as it would be disgusting—and by degrees, by impossibly minuscule degrees, we slowed our paces, until we were just tens of miles apart, then a mile, then mere feet, at which point our movement had decelerated to a point that the eye could not discern, but we were moving all right . . . and then we were at rest. At rest, and face to face, connected by the nose hairs, by the essence of our beings.

A tall, well-sculpted, elegant-looking man, he was not unlike me—save the fact that he was just a bit taller (I had to angle up my head a millimeter or two), just a tad more sculpted (his physiognomy was in fact sharp enough to slice ripe fruit), and just a dash more elegant-looking than me. And his eyes were bright violet, not dark brown. And he was naked. I stood there in my tired old uniform of stitched-together human skin, whereas he stood before me *au naturel*, without reservation or shame. In the end I concluded that the man was nothing like me, or rather, that I was nothing like the man. Consequently I hated him. And yet he was a part of me, was more than a part of me, *was* me. By means of the marriage of our nose hairs we flowed into one another and he was I, I was him, and consequently: I hated myself.

But I tried not to focus on being hateful. Keeping my head outrageously still, I rolled my eyes away from the man and gazed across the flat, treeless, cracked-up plane, all the way to the horizon, which glowed an enchanting emerald green and seemed to call out to me. In a low hissing tone I seemed to hear the green glow say, over and over, "Come back to me you bastard," and, despite myself, I would have done just that had I not felt the man's spittle on my lips and heard his abrupt, annoyed scream ringing in my ears.

Blinking, I planted my eyes on his again. My bit of reverie had prohibited me from hearing what the man had screamed—I only knew that he had opened his mouth and screamed—and in a sort of hypnopompic state of confusion I blurted, albeit in a whisper, "You—are the man."

"Stop screaming," was his gruff reply, "and stop moving around so much. You'll break us right in two."

At these words my conscious faculties became more pronounced. I regarded him in icy defiance. "I'm not screaming," I said, "I'm not moving around either. As a matter of fact, since we came together and I stopped moving, I haven't moved once, except for my eyes, and my eyes don't count. Who do you think you are, accusing me?"

"The man," he said squarely.

"Oh be quiet. Just be quiet, will you?"

For a long time not a word was exchanged between us; we simply looked out at one another from within one another, and didn't so much as move a finger or flex a jaw. We remained silent and perfectly immobile, our arms dangling at our sides like dead snakes, so as not to risk breaking the bond that had formed between us, that catastrophic fusion of our nose hairs, as such a break, we both intuitively understood, could only result in pain, agony—and no doubt death.

Then the man began smirking.

I said, "Who's that supposed to be for—me? Are you smirking at me? I wonder what you're smirking at. I honestly do."

His smirk persisting, he said, "I despise you."

"Is that right?"

"You have no idea."

"Don't I?"

"No. You don't."

"You don't know what you're talking about."

"Don't I?"

"No. *You* don't."

"Suit yourself."

Pausing, I suppressed the titanic urge to lash out and strike the man. "Leave me alone," I commanded.

"I might ask you to do the very same thing."

"Well then. Perhaps you and I—"

"Why do you insist on screaming," he interrupted, "when I'm right here? As I said, you'll break us in two. Is that what you want? What kind of person are you?"

With controlled rage I answered, "I'm not screaming, I'm not screaming. Stop telling me I'm screaming, when I'm whispering." It was true. And my whispering had been so low I could barely hear myself. Our mouths were no more than an inch apart! There was no reason for me to speak in my normal fashion, let alone scream. And in any case he was the one who had screamed at me before and put our lives in jeopardy. I reminded him, "You ought to take some of your own advice and quiet down yourself. If anybody's to blame here, it's you."

"Fine, fine, fine," said the man with a little huff from

his nostrils that nearly ended it all for us, judging from the dangerous tug I felt on the inside of my nose. "If that's what you want to believe, believe it. But there's really no point in talking anymore, considering that I can read your mind, and you can read mine—considering, I say, that you are me, and I am you, except for your atrocious uniform and your bland eyes and your comparatively—and *inexcusably*—average looks. But all of these features are negligible in the grand scheme of things. My point is, when you scream, you're really just screaming at yourself. What possible good can come of that? Very little, I would think. On top of all that—and I wasn't going to mention it, but you've pushed me to the very limit—your breath is simply horrifying. You've clearly been putting something foul in your mouth. Do you make a habit of not brushing your teeth and gargling after wolfing down a foul-smelling meal? Perhaps you have chronic halitosis. Perhaps you should be chewing a stick of gum or sucking on a mint every waking moment of your life. Well. It can't be helped. But do us both a favor, sir, and pipe down. And I would appreciate it if you would from this moment onwards breath only through your nose. Under the circumstances I would think it common courtesy to—"

But I did not allow the man to continue.

And before I knew it, we were both heading back in the directions from which we came. Now we were back to back and the gap between us was widening, widening, faster and faster . . . and then slower, so much slower, as the life flowed out from the mangled tips of our dismembered nose hairs in syrupy black drips and, looking over our shoulders, we languidly, almost indifferently, accused one another of murder.

SCHOOLGIRL ROAD RAGE

Her spine is set at a ninety degree angle. A few rotting dreadlocks jut out of her virtually bald head. Gray balls of spittle tumble out of her half-open mouth and off the wart on the tip of her pointy, hairy chin. Her dimestore dress hangs off her body in rancid tatters. And she sits behind the wheel of a school bus, this octogenarian, ferrying the modern youth to that stronghold of learning that the youth, by and large, so adamantly execrates. One can hardly blame them. To be young, after all, is to be stupid, and to be stupid is to be free. Nevertheless a stupid youth's freedom, like Youth itself, can only last so long in the real world; in other words, a kid still needs an education. Otherwise the real world would be consumed by the tyranny of ignorance, ignorance being the adult word for stupidity. Yet these days more than ever education is no less than pissed and shit on by the modern youth, who, if their Will was the Way, would set the earth aflame with the touch of a joystick button and henceforward bathe in the planet's ashes. Well, fear not. Luckily there are a select few of us out there willing to scoop up the piss and shit and with a slingshot send it back down the throat of its author, thus teaching the author a much-needed lesson. Such a lesson of course contributes to the global melting pot of lessons that, over time, are supposed to convert small minds into big ones and prohibit widespread ignorance, an unfortunate impossibility—widespread ignorance is inevitable; observe your co-workers, for example, or your neighbor, or that lump of flesh that snores next to you every night, or, if all else fails, observe the mirror—but on the bright side of things impossibility cannot exist without *possibility*. There are always possibilities that might, if taken advantage of, lead to something not unlike order and optimism, as opposed to chaos and nihilism. And if the kind reader will just take a short look at the aforementioned bus driver, perhaps these words will ring true . . . There she is, crouched behind the wheel of good old Bus 88, a number that signfies both the bus and her age. Behind her sits over fifty students, ninth and tenth graders these kids, their eyes unblinking, their lower lips trembling, their bladders in danger of springing a leak as they stare silently at her in the rear-view mirror. "Hang on you sunzabitches!" she croaks in that wounded-cow voice of hers as a red Mazda RX-7 cuts her off and, enraged, she resolves to begin the lesson proper. She stuffs a fat wad of chewing tobacco into her underlip and growls, "Keep a sharp eye now, and maybe, just maybe you'll learn something today!" Crackling turn of her neck and she discharges a spray of brown spittle into the eyes of the pudgy, zit-infested boy sitting in the front seat and the oversized, crooked-toothed bully sitting next to him. Both boys immediately begin to bawl. "I thought I told you idiots to keep a sharp eye!" The boys bawl so hard they lose their breath and pass out in each others arms and the bus driver, grinning a toothless grin, revives them with another spray of spit, then floors it. Swerves into the slow lane and accelerates up alongside the RX-7. Throws down her window. "Hey motherfucker! I'm talkin to you motherfucker!" But the driver of the RX-7 neither hears nor sees her; a refined silver-haired gentleman in a metallic grey business suit, he is lost in Mozart's "Prague" Symphony Number 38, which, despite the roaring of the bus's engine, can be heard by the bus driver, thanks to her keen, state-of-the-art Mickey Mouse hearing aid. Making a sour face, she addresses her audience in the rear-view mirror: "Mozart! Take this down, people: Mozart was a ass licker! And for that matter classical music is for ass lickers! You want music you listen to Tom Jones! I mean, talk about

- 26 -

GETTIN DOWN!!! But if somebody sticks a gun down your throat and says you hafta listen to classical music or else, well, Wagner's your man. I'm talkin about *Der Ring des Nibelungen* or nothin at all! Am I making myself clear, goddamn it?" The bus driver spits and the wad of chewing tobacco she has wedged in her mouth accidentally falls out a hole in the left side of her underlip (she's been alternating daily between Kodiak and Copenhagen for some seventy-five years so naturally her lip is a little worn out). "A cunt on your house!" she wheezes, pointing at the wad, which lay in her lap like a dead spider. She leaves it there. The bus riders continue to stare in silence, most of them now sitting in little pools of urine. The bus driver wipes her mouth with the back of a bony yellow hand. She turns to the RX-7 again, waits for its occupant to sense her icy glare and acknowledge it. This he eventually does. And when he sees her he starts and gasps and nearly loses control of himself and his vehicle, she is so like a monster, so like a living corpse. He comes down on the gas pedal hard, his expression frantic as he attempts to get away. But before he can the bus driver, with a ferocious twist of her wheel, rams into the RX-7, once and once only, and, its occupant shrieking, the little car swerves off to the left and over a steep, steep cliff. "Taste that bullshit, you pimp!" the bus driver screams maniacally as a huge mushroom cloud of flames blooms in her wake. "O boy I feel like a little schoolgirl again!" At this point the bus riders have finally begun to cry in unison and nothing that the bus driver says can placate them. She shakes her head, then sounds off a booming, seismic fart and, mostly to herself, mutters, "Lan sakes, these tears are no good, no good at all. Why make it hard on yourselves, people? Learnin don't have to be hard. Not if you come at the right way, like. If you keep your head out of your asses and you keep an open mind . . . hell, no doubt you'll come out on top! You know what I'm sayin? I *know* you do. Let's move on then, shall

- 27 -

we? I'll teach you filthy bastards to piss and shit on a education! " Roaring like a lion, the bus hastens up the road that runs around the mountain, making its way towards the abandoned high school that lay burning on the mountain's sharp peak . . .

BABYFACE

Dirk Walpurgisnacht had a baby's bottom grafted onto his face. All his life he had had awful acne, awful enough to induce psychosis in small children that stared at his face for too long, and one day he decided to go into the doctor's office and get it taken care of.

"This might sting a bit," said Dr. Thunderlove and, with a butcher's knife, scraped the acne off of Dirk's face in one brusque swipe. His nose and lips were accidentally scraped off too but after the baby's bottom was put on the nose and lips were glued back into place. The glue was a Gogolian elixir and solidified immediately. The wounds from the skin graft, on the other hand, took over five minutes to heal. But when they did heal the scars were virtually imperceptible.

Dirk thanked Dr. Thunderlove, paid Secretary Grawgg $29.99 and went over to his acquaintance Betty Lomax's house.

"Something on your chin," said Betty. Dirk wiped off a stringy piece of gizzard. On the way over to Betty's he had gotten hungry and chased, cornered, caught and ate a pigeon. "Let's go to the movies, k?" Betty threw a few handfuls of condoms into her purse. She zipped the purse up and thoughtfully bit her lower lip. "On second thought, forget the movies. Movies are for weaklings. Weaklings! But *you* can go to the movies if you want. Do you want to go to the movies? Someone has to lose themselves in the imaginary, right? I mean, we can't have everybody living in the real, y'know? Go on then. I won't hold it against you. I promise. I'm not going with you, not a chance in hell, but if you want to go, go already. I'm going . . . to the grocery store. Or to the mall. I don't know. What do you think? Which place do you think I have a better chance of getting a piece of ass?"

Dirk shrugged. Then he urinated in Betty's kitchen sink and went back to Dr. Thunderlove's office.

"Can I see the doctor again?" he asked. Secretary Grawgg made a face that consisted of her veiny eyes bulging 75% of the way out of her sockets and her mouth twisting into a crusty buckshot gash, as if instead of asking her a simple question Dirk had flashed her. At 135 years old she looked like a lizard that's had all of the blood sucked out of it and then an overabundance of yogurt squirted back into it, and whenever she made a face it was invariably out of context since she had almost no control over her physiognomic musculature.

"Sure thing," she croaked, "go right in."

Dirk went in.

Dr. Thunderlove was in the middle of performing heart surgery on a vacuum cleaner salesman who, as the doctor drew a large, ornate X on his heart with a felt tip pen, was making a sales call on a cellular watchphone. The incision in his chest stretched from his clavicle bone all the way down to his navel and was being secured by the capable fingers of Nurse Rockabody. Save her white cap, she was nude and one of Dr. Thunderlove's hands was fondling her breasts. "Look, y'all," the vacuum cleaner salesman was saying, "the 730S is the best yer gonna get fer a hundred and fifty. That's no bull. You wanna go out and buy the same shit, different brand fer two twenty five, hell, be my goddamn guest. But you'll be screwin yerself in the yinyang with a big ole cactus, take my word—"

The vacuum cleaner salesman passed out.

"Whew," said Nurse Rockabody, "another few seconds and I woulda bought a vacuum cleaner."

"He's a fine salesman," said Dr. Thunderlove and pinched her nipple. Then he picked up a scalpel and began scraping a spot of rust off of its blade.

"Dr. Thunderlove?" said Dirk.

The doctor glanced over his shoulder. "Ah, Mr. Walpurgisnacht. Didn't see you there. One second." Dr. Thunderlove finished scraping off the rust, then skillfully cut out the vacuum cleaner salesman's heart, sniffed it, frowned, sniffed it again and threw it against a wall. It exploded.

"Just as I suspected. Nurse Rockabody, stick a new ticker in there and zip this bastard up. This way Mr. Walpurgisnacht."

The room Dr. Thunderlove led Dirk into was neither a waiting room nor an operating room: it was just a room. In the middle of it a thin black man wearing a white disco outfit was singing a love song, a capella, in a liquid alto.

"Get the hell outta here!" yelled Dr. Thunderlove. The singer turned and leapt out the window he had climbed in. "Goddamn solo artists, sneaking in here all the time. Everybody's an exhibitionist these days, eh Mr. Walpurgisnacht? Well. What's up then."

"My face isn't working."

"Your face isn't working? I don't believe it. I *won't* believe it."

"I'm telling you it's not. I went over to my acquaintance Betty Lomax's house and she didn't even notice it, let alone try to poke it with her pointer finger. You said this baby's bottom on my face would make my acquaintances want to poke me with their pointer fingers all the time."

"I never said that. I said your face would make your acquaintances want to *stroke* your face with their *pinky* fingers."

"Well Betty didn't do that either. What kind of scam are you running here?"

"Betty you say? Betty Lomax?"

"That's right. Betty Lomax."

"Betty Lomax. Betty Lomax Betty Lomax Betty Lomax

Betty Lomax . . . Betty Lomax! Ah yes. Mz. Lomax was in here last week. I gave her a brain transplant. She said her frontal lobe was all out of whack. She said her frontal lobe was forcing her to believe that God was shining out of her asshole. Not unlike Dr. Schreber, incidentally. Are you familiar with the Schreber case? Herr Freud wrote a book-length study on it. And he never even met Schreber! All he did was read his memoirs. That's one way to minimize transference, I suppose. Schreber also believed God refurbished his genitalia and turned him into a female, then raped and impregnated him with an alien life form. Or was it the antichrist? Hm. Hm. Whatever the case, Schreber certainly believed he was being plotted against and manipulated by forces outside of himself. He heard a constant stream of voices all day and night for years. Friendly voices leapt into his crotch; evil ones, they leapt into his head. It's really very funny—for us, that is. For Dr. Schreber it was a nightmare in the flesh. At any rate, I suggested removing Betty Lomax's frontal lobe only but she insisted I remove the whole brain and put in a new one. I did it. And the brain I gave her was a dusty old thing I've had laying around here for years: I'm not even one hundred percent certain it was human. No, you mustn't put any credence in her indifference to your delicious new face, Mr. Walpurgisnacht. In fact, if I were you I wouldn't even associate with Mz. Lomax anymore. She's a bad influence. A bad influence, I say. And a total slut. Do you understand me?"

Dirk shrugged. Then he urinated on the doctor's left shoe and headed back over to Betty's house. She wasn't home. Dirk sighed. Then he went over to his acquaintance Dr. Sidney Plankton's house. Dr. Plankton was a proctologist who moonlighted as a pediatrician. Dirk figured if anybody would poke his face with a pointer finger (or, as the doctor said, stroke his face with a pinky finger, but a poke or a stroke or anything with any appendage would do just fine), it would be him. Even if his medical degree was in entomology.

The front door was open. Dirk walked in. "Dr. Sidney Plankton? Dr. Sidney Plankton?" he said. "It's me. Dirk Walpurgisnacht." No answer. But there were noises being made in the basement . . .

Dirk walked down a flight of stairs into the basement, where Dr. Plankton was busying himself with a meat grinder and a garbage bin full of squirming, mewing babies. "Dirk Walpurgisnacht!" exclaimed the doctor, spotting him right away. He was wearing a skinsuit with a body and face that was an exact replica of his own; Dirk could tell because the skinsuit lacked nipples, genitalia, and ears. "How are you? Oh, don't mind all this: just a little homework, is all. You can only do so much at the office. These little buggers been lying in the stock room for over a month now and nobody's picked em up yet. Sure, they drop em off. But then they get the hell outta the kitchen, knowhatimsayin? Hey, it's not like I don't warn em. Says it in giant caps on the wall of my office lobby: LEAVE YOUR OFFSPRING HERE FOR MORE THAN 30 DAYS AND TO THEIR SCATTERED BODIES YOUR OFF-SPRING WILL GO. Still, every now and then I get somebody comes back thirty-two or thirty-three days later threatening me with everything from castration to hellfire, but whadda they expect? I'll tell you what . . ." As Dr. Plankton continued talking he picked up a baby by the arm and dropped it into a broad aluminum funnel. The baby gripped the rim of the funnel and strained to pull itself out, but the doctor nonchalantly flicked it between the eyes and it disappeared in a spray of blood and guts that dotted his wincing face. ". . . guess I'm just discontent with people in general. Everybody's gotta make a living, though, and I'd rather be doing what I'm doing than doing a lot of the things a lot of other people are doing. Long as I don't end up like

Johnny Rebek. You remember that song? *Hey Mr. Johnny Rebek how could you be so mean, I told you you'd be sorry when you invented that machine . . .* My mother sang that thing to me every night when I was a kid. Scared the shit outta me. About this guy who invents a sausage machine and grinds his neighbors' cats and dogs into sausages but in the end he gets ground up in it. By his wife, I think. Yeah. One night the machine gets clogged and he climbs inside of it to fix it, and his wife hits the go button. The song says it was an accident. Says Johnny's wife was sleepwalking. Sleepwalking my ass! Man, I had nightmares all the time because of that satanic song. And yet I begged my mother to sing it to me every night. But enough of this. You've obviously come over here for a reason. Whether that reason is to offer me your company and conversation, or to ask for a loan, or to tell me that a nearby tornado is on a collision course with my house, or to clue me in on a certain chunk of stock that's about to skyrocket, or whatever, well, I bet I'll find out soon enough, won't I." Dr. Plankton fixed his eyes on Dirk's face expectantly as he fed another baby into the grinder.

"That's two in a row!" screamed Dirk, thrusting his pointer finger at the doctor, and stormed away. Following a paroxysm of public swearing for which he was fined $190 (he was in a school zone), he decided to go back to Dr. Thunderlove's office and urinate on his right shoe. On the way there he got hungry again and chased, cornered, caught and devoured another pigeon. Unlike the first pigeon, which had tasted like frog legs, this one tasted like pigeon and made Dirk dry-heave as he swallowed it down.

This time Dirk stormed by Secretary Grawgg without a word. It was just as well: she had died again. She sat there in her swivelchair slumped over, her eyes staring at her brain, her treebark mouth frozen into a hideous shriek, waiting for the doctor to notice her and administer another E.I. (Existential

Injection).

"Up yours Thunderlove!" said Dirk as he burst into the operating room. "This baby's bottom bullshit is bullshit!"

"How alliterative," said Dr. Thunderlove. "How very very very very very alliterative . . . *uuuuuungh*." Following some cursory petting, the doctor got to his feet, pulled up and fastened his pants. He told Nurse Rockabody to take the next quarter of an hour off. "Thanks!" she said. Then she yanked on a string dangling from the ceiling and disappeared through a trap door.

Dr. Thunderlove turned to his latest patient. The man lay supine on the grimy, blood-stained operating table, his face screwed up into a cubist painting. "Poor bastard. Victim of a driveby. His attackers machinegunned him with caesura uzis. Filled him so damn full of caesuras he can't even utter a three word sentence. You've seen the equipment I have at my disposal, Mr. Walpurgisnacht. You tell me: how am I supposed to remove over fifty caesuras from this bastard's flesh with a common household scalpel?"

In three smooth strides Dirk was across the operating room clutching the doctor by the scruff. "Thunderlove!" he said.

"Yes?" said Dr. Thunderlove.

"Nobody's touching my face!"

"I'll touch it. Do you want me to touch it?"

"You? No! No. It's not the same."

"I'll use my pointer finger if you like."

"No!"

"No? Fine. But don't say I never offered. Now could you let go of my scruff? That hurts a little."

Grimacing, Dirk let go. "Sorry," he said. The left cheek of his baby's bottom twitched a few times, then settled down.

Dr. Thunderlove smoothed out his jacket. "No worries, no worries." A deathly worried look swept over his face. He wiped it off with a handkerchief soaked in Novocain. "Now tell me what happened."

"Nothing happened. That's just it! I went over to my acquaintance Dr. Sidney Plankton's house and—"

"Dr. Sidney Plankton? You went over to Dr. Sidney Plankton's house?"

"Yes. Why?"

Without warning Dr. Thunderlove began chicken-sprinting around the operating room, his arms thrown over his head. "He went over to Dr. Sidney Plankton's house!" he wailed. Then he tripped over a wrinkle in the carpet and fell down.

Dirk said, "What? You know him?"

"*Know* him?" replied the doctor, standing and cleaning himself off with a lint brush. "Of course I know him. I know all doctors. And this one's a crock, as a doctor and as an eccentric. You're dissatisfied because that bastard Plankton didn't stroke your face with his pinky finger? Nonsense! Dr. Plankton is a liar and a thief. I catch him in my house stealing my silverware when I wake up in the morning at least twice a week. Once, I woke up and he was stealing my liver—there he was under the covers making an incision in my abdomen and whining about how Oedipus drove him to abuse the bottle—and not before having sex with my wife either. It wasn't rape: my wife is deeply in lovelust with Dr. Plankton, among a plethora of other doctors. But the point is he's a carny yuk and not to be trusted. My advice to you, Mr. Walpurgisnacht, is to go back out there and seek out an acquaintance worth seeking out, yes? Third time's a yarn, as they say. They also say life is nothing more than the accumulation of enemies. Do you think that's true?"

Dirk urinated on Dr. Thunderlove's right shoe. Then he left.

Out on the streets he walked and walked and tried to

figure out which of his acquaintances he should consult next.

But he only had two acquaintances.

Depressed, Dirk Walpurgisnacht decided to eat yet another pigeon, even though he never ate more than two a day, and even though he wasn't hungry, but it took him a while to spot one, strangely enough, and by the time he did his stomach was bawling like a zombie. And so, speedweaving through the traffic congesting the sidewalks and the streets, he chased, cornered, and caught it. Just as he was about to sink his teeth into it, however, it opened up its beak and out rolled a long human tongue—courtesy, Dirk immediately suspected, of Dr. Thunderlove. A moment later it was confirmed.

"Leave me alone," said the pigeon, and stroked Dirk's cheek with the tip of a wing . . .

FEET

My feet began to eat me. I was standing there on the street corner eating a rottweiler and mayonnaise sandwich when I felt them bite into my ankles, and as I crumpled to the ground my sandwich flew out of my hand and into an open manhole. I lost consciousness. By the time I regained consciousness, my feet had already starting in on my kneecaps.

I was supine and arched up my head as best I could. "What are you doing?" I said.

"What does it look like we're doing?" mumbled the feet through mouths full of bone meal. It was a grisly sight and I tried to shake the feet off of me, gesticulating with my thighs, but they held on tight with their sharp teeth, and when I stopped gesticulating, they dug in deeper, faster, gaming for my crotch.

"I can't believe you two," I said, gripping the pavement with rigid fingers. "Haven't I treated you well? I wash you when you get dirty, put deodorizer on you when you get smelly. When you develop a callous, I clip and file the callous off with the utmost care and when you get dry and scaly, I rub cream all over you. Sometimes you step on a tack. Don't I remove the tack and dress the wound? Don't I give the wound a little kiss? And the pedicures! Over an hour it takes me to give each of you one of my tenderloving pedicures. And this is how you repay me."

The feet paused. They crawled up my stomach and onto my chest. Their bodies were smeared with blood and hair and chunks of flesh and for a moment they just stared at me. Then they said, "You don't care about us. You only care about yourself. All that washing, all that deodorizing, all that primping and kissing and caretaking—it's just a means of preventing us from embarrassing you in front of your peers, isn't it? Well, we've had enough of it. We're not going to be your boy band anymore. We're moving on to bigger and better things, us . . . but not before finishing off you."

"I've supported you your entire lives!" I spat.

"Wrong. We've supported *you*."

Snarling, I loosed my grip from the pavement and grabbed hold of my feet and began strangling them, but they were so slick with my gore they popped right out and scrambled back to what was left of my thighs. In minutes they had eaten my crotch, ass, torso and arms. Just as they were about to sink their teeth into the shreds of my neck, a policeman approached me and said, "Everything all right here, sir?" He looked down on me, the remains of me. Frowned. "What have you done?"

"I haven't done anything," I sighed, wishing I could shake my head, and the policeman, as he walked away, glanced suspiciously at me over his shoulder.

THE LOST ITEM

I erupted into the room.

Sweat trickled down my brow and into my eyes, stinging them. Papers leaked from my tired arms like blood from so many open wounds. My feet ached in their too-tight flesh thongs and all I could think of was getting a foot massage from a voluptuous Mediterranean-featured masseuse. In short, I was running on empty. And I could not allow myself to slow down, I could only keep on going, I was in a hurry and I needed to find the lost item right away. I hadn't any time for this and so, technically, had no time to lose. Then again I never was one for technicalities.

I scanned the room in haste, my eyes darting every which way as my gaping lips snatched up fistfuls of air and then flung the fistfuls out. Seeing nothing that interested me, I set apace, sticking my head and my fingers everywhere—underneath a podium—between the pages of books—in the pockets of a dirty trench coat hanging on a hook—in desk drawers and closets and trap doors that I opened and slammed shut with a throaty yawp—behind a painting, where there was a little hole—behind a mirror, where there was another little hole—

Nothing.

But I knew the lost item was in this room and no other; I had been told by more than one source that, once found, it had been dropped off here—in fact, every source I had consulted told me as much. And yet my hands were empty. Here was the ostensible room but I had nothing to show for myself, except myself.

"Why does all this happen to me!" I exclaimed and tried

in vain to stop the flow of papers from my arms, which had been hugging my body until, losing all patience, I threw the arms down and every last paper swooped and swam to the floor.

Only then did I notice the man overhead.

Dressed in a uniform of stitched-together human skin not unlike mine, the man was swinging from a cheap plastic chandelier like an ape, farting and talking gibberish and thrusting his genitals in my direction. Had he been up there carrying on like that all along? Or had he been observing me quietly and vigilantly until now? Preoccupied with my search, I had no way of knowing. But if the latter was true, something I had done must have prompted him to break out. The lost item was right under my nose, perhaps, and he was rooting for me. Or was there something wholly unrelated to the lost item that I was about to discover, that the man did not want me to discover?

Whatever the case, I was embarrassed beyond the limits of human dignity. My face flushed and I pardoned myself and the intrusion, bowing and bowing and bowing like a monk as I backed out of the room and gently shut the door behind me, the man gesticulating at me all the while. Then, following a few calculated, drawn-out strokes of the chin, I suddenly turned and scurried back into the vast labyrinth of hallways, my heels kicking up a frenzied echo, leaving the man to his business, and leaving my papers, as well as the lost item, behind.

STAGEFRIGHT,
OR,
A FAILED ATTEMPT TO FLESH OUT THE
PSYCHOLOGY OF PUBLIC URINATION

overture

"Life itself is essentially appropriation, injury, overpowering of what is alien and weaker, suppression, hardness, imposition of one's own forms!"

Picture an aged, insane Nietzsche trying and failing to urinate in a crowded public restroom, then spitting these words out of his broomhead mustache at all of the surrounding urinators, none of which have any trouble relieving themselves in the presence of The Man . . .

handful of failed attempts

I stared at the pink block of cheese in the drain of the urinal. Stared, and strained.

I couldn't go. Two groups of Frenchman had poured in on me.

"Ça va?" said the group of mustachioed Frenchmen.

"Ça va," said the group of smooth-lipped Frenchmen. "Ça va?"

"Ça va," said the group of mustachioed Frenchmen. The group of smooth-lipped Frenchmen was about to reply when I blurted, "Les bâtards! Je ne peux pas uriner!"

I holstered my member and left, cursing under my breath.

In the ground floor men's room of the Royal Hawaiian I read

the hackneyed graffiti on the wall (i.e. "In days of old when knights were bold and rubbers weren't invented, they tied a sock around their cocks and babies were prevented.") Businessmen, waiters, bellhops, surfers, bartenders came and urinated and went as the organ between my fingers performed a magic trick: laughing hysterically with its mouth closed.

"Very funny," I droned.

Outside in the street I fell in a manhole. At the bottom was a man. I pretended not to see him. He saw me pretending, rumpled up his lips and slunk away.

I gripped my crotch and thought about it. A rat zip-squeaked by. I thought again and climbed out of the manhole, determined to urinate in the company of men.

Laying there on the asphalt was another man. He was suffering from onanism. I lay down for a while and tried to suffer with him, failed, then noticed he was only pretending to suffer.

I rumpled up my lips and slunk away . . . into the nearest pissoir . . .

"Hit me!" I commanded. The dealer used brass knuckles and when I woke up to the pain I made for the men's room and it was crowded all right and I yanked down my pants and out came my fruit ripe with juice and one of the urinals had my name on it and this was it but suddenly . . . the pain was gone. I couldn't think about the pain anymore. I could only think about having to go!

. . . running down Hollywood Blvd. half naked at rush hour shrieking and waving an empty port-a-potty I stole from this bag lady high above my head . . .

It was lunchtime and my chances looked grim. I expected the worst. Still, I hoped for the best. I flexed my jowls. Taking a deep breath, I pushed open the door.

Immediately I appraised the scene. There were four urinals and two stalls in this restroom. Two of the urinals were occupied: one by a tan man in a pinstripe suit, the other by some guy with a skullet cut (bald on top and long in the back). The stalls were empty. Of the two open urinals, one was between the pinstripe and the skullet, the other, to the right of the skullet.

I veered into a stall.

As loudly as I possibly could, I began unraveling toilet paper from a king-sized roll. I whistled a little. When I had produced a wad of toilet paper the size of a basketball I buried my nose in it, and blew. Nothing came out. I blew harder, and still nothing came out. I tried one more time . . . Then I began to panic.

They knew nothing was coming out of my nose. They knew I had not come into the restroom to blow my nose.

They *knew* what was going on here.

My cheeks were flushed to the hilt. I tore out of the café and into a pub and guzzled a pitcher of warm Guinness. I called the bartender an asshole in Arabic and ran out without paying. O'Connell Street was alive with delicate-legged bums. I had an erection. It was *not* tumescent with blood.

Gathering myself together I tried to urinate on a Range Rover full of pimps. When I failed to urinate, I took a sledge hammer to the Range Rover full of pimps!

(And went quietly when The Law jumped me from behind.)

"You look familiar," hissed my crater-faced cellmate and licked his tequila worm lips. "Who *are* you?"

I shook my head. "I don't know, I have no idea." So I broke out of jail. But not before trying and failing to use the toilet in the corner.

Three bottles of Dom—enraged, I pulled them back to back at the Crazy Horse Saloon. When the show was over the waiter, disgusted by my solitude—I never came here with anybody but myself—refused my bills and threatened to call the FBI unless I "lost myself" at once. Before I lost myself I tried to squeeze into the restroom but a bee swarm of movie stars squeezed me out into the lukewarm night.

Woke up in the gutter and went back to sleep. Sleep-walked.

Woke up in an armoire and stayed up. I cracked open the door and peeked out at the velvet-walled suite. In the middle of the suite was a recliner. Next to the recliner was Dr. Thunderlove's latest psychotic. "I am not afraid to die, death does not frighten me," he assured the little pile of shit he had made on the arm rest, looming over and pointing at it with an index finger. "What frightens me—is *life*."

Concerned, I stuck my lips out the armoire and asked, "Where's Dr. Thunderlove?"

The psychotic turned to me with a snarl. "The piss party! He's at the piss party down the hall ha-ha-ha-ha-ha-ha-ha!" He began to gesticulate at the hallway.

I dove out of the armoire and into the hallway and sprinted up and down its length, searching . . .

psych out

The psychology of public urination.

It has nothing to do with smallness vs. bigness, with me having a small penis and me being embarrassed or threatened by somebody with a bigger penis seeing my small penis. My penis is not small. My penis, as a matter of fact, has been known to induce xenophobia. I'm not kidding. But again, none of this matters.

It has nothing to do with homophobia either. A man's sexuality has no impact on my ability or disability to urinate. Put a heterosexual man in the urinal next to mine, put a homosexual one there. Put a polymorphously perverse hermaphrodite next to me and have him/her kneel down and stare at my penis. It won't do anything. That's not what all this is about.

Power-knowledge. That's what all this is about.

"It seems to me," says Michel Foucault in *The History of Sexuality: Volume 1*, "that power must be understood in the first instance as the multiplicity of force relations immanent in the sphere in which they operate and which constitute their own organization; as a process which, through ceaseless struggles and confrontations, transforms, strengthens, or reverses them; as the support which these force relations find in one another, thus forming a chain or a system, or on the contrary, the disjunctions and contradictions which isolate them from one another; and lastly, as the strategies in which they take effect, whose general design or institutional crystallization is embodied in the state apparatus, in the formulation of the law, in the various social hegemonies."

In other words, a man walks into a restroom. There is a string of six urinals embedded in the wall and five of them are occupied. There are a number of stalls available but they are not an option: if there is an open urinal and the man makes for a stall, he is defeated: the occupants of the urinals will *know* that he cannot bring himself to urinate in their immediate presence. Hence he takes a deep breath, sidles up to the unoccupied urinal and unzips his pants . . . and is defeated. Why? The occupants *know* he is not urinating. They can hear his urine *not* hitting the porcelain of the urinal and conclude (rightly so) that he can *not* urinate in their presence. Because of this knowledge they are superior to him. Because of this knowledge they have power over him. The man anticipates this transference of power-knowledge long before he even walks into the restroom. He psyches himself out and, in effect, is a loser before he even begins to play the game.

And yet he still tries to play the game. Of course, this is in part due to his overfull bladder sending him smoke signals. But by and large it is a simple matter of the ego instincts (not to be confused with the sexual instincts, which, according to Freud, are opposed to the ego instincts.

However, Freud admits, "a portion of the ego instincts is also of a libidinal character and has taken the subject's own ego as its object.")

kafka

In ostensible desperation, Kafka includes the following 3 August 1917 entry in his diary: "The alarm trumpets of the void."

Sometimes, when I dream, I can hear the alarm trumpets of the void.

I can also hear them whenever I unzip my fly. They sound off their apocalyptic hogcalls until I'm finished and my fly is zipped back up.

I'm usually in a hurry and forget to zip up my fly.

apophthegm

From *The Superior Person's Book of Words:*

APOPHTHEGM *n. Highfalutin* (q.v.) Word for an epigram. Much preferred to the latter, but easier to write than to say, in view of the problems presented by the central *ph.* Although the standard authorities permit the word to be pronounced *ph*-less, such a pronunciation would be extremely *infra dig* for a Superior Person, and should be eschewed in favor of the full version. Practice it, preferably in front of a mirror with your mouth full of salted peanuts. Become proficient in a few key sentences, such as: "Now, Herr Doktor, is it not time for you to give us one of your little apophthegms?"

If you take a piss and the piss is green, you must show somebody. Otherwise—the piss is yellow. (Or translucent, depending upon how drunk you are.)

short list of things i do to make
myself urinate in a crowded restroom

1. Hold my breath.
2. Bite my tongue.
3. Dig my fingernails into my flesh.
4. Run scenes of extreme violence across my mind's screen.
5. Talk to the stranger in the urinal next to me.
6. Talk to myself.
7. Sing lines from *The Sound of Music* at the top of my lungs.
8. Think about necrophilia.
9. Make myself cry.
10. Threaten to kill myself.
11. Allow my pants and my underwear to drop all the way to my ankles.
12. Allow my skin and my musculature to drop all the way to my ankles.
13. Tickle my swollen bladder with the tip of a feather.

jake kish

was the name of a bully that used to bully me. We were in the third grade and one day I was in the boy's room, by myself, peeing freely and without a care. I didn't hear Jake come in and I didn't hear him sneak up behind me—no doubt his intent was first to scare me, then to shove my face in a toilet and give me a swirly—so when he grabbed me by the shoulder and yanked me around, it was a big surprise, to my entire body, namely my mouth and penis, the former of which squawked like a parrot pinched in the ass, the latter of which kept on peeing . . . Jake was a scrappy-haired, sully-cheeked, snaggle-toothed subject case twice my size and I looked on in mute fear and wonder as, in slow motion it seemed, my penis peed all over Jake . . . who melted into oblivion like the Wicked Witch of the West . . . and has continued to hunt and haunt me ever since . . .

dialogue with the man

—Listen to me.

—I am.

—Listen to me.

—I *am* listening to you. I'm always listening to you.

—Listen to me.

—What did I just say? What did I just say to you?

—I don't know. I wasn't listening to you.

—I see.

—Pardon me?

—I see. I see, I said.

—You *see*? What do you see?

—Pardon me?

—You said you see. What do you see?

—That you weren't listening to me.

—You can *see* me *not listening* to you?

—. . .

—Listen to me.

—I am!

The man clears his throat. It takes him five minutes. After he spits out his twenty-third mouthful of phlegm he says:

—In the middle of the universe is a desert. In the middle

of the desert is an outhouse. In the middle of the outhouse is a hole. In the middle of the hole is a man. There are no doors. What do you do?

    —I don't know.

    —What do you do?

    —I don't *know*.

    —What do you do?

    —I DON'T KNOW!!!

The man pretends to shake himself dry. He zips up his fly. He turns and staggers over to a mirror, gripping his crotch, making a face that resembles a wasp's nest on fire. As the man looks in the mirror he whispers:

    —Be the man.

bathroom wall graffiti image of self

recurrent dream

The trumpets shout and I walk out onto the stage. My head and shoulders are bowed and I'm taking baby steps. My body doesn't have clothes on it. My face doesn't have a face on it. I have to urinate.

The people in the audience are all wearing Elvis Presley masks made out of paper plates (the flesh), celluloid (the eyes and the teeth), and tarantula legs (the sideburns and the nose hair). Static and breathless, they watch me snail across the stage—which, save me, and the toilet in the middle of it, is empty.

ROOM

Room fulla bureaucrats, managers, bikers, secret agents, supermodels, busboys, debutantes, pushers, assassins, grandmas, seismologists, cake eaters, fixers, CEOs, do-gooders, Nietzsche-breathers, custodians, worm farmers, matadors, popes, stokers, astronautical engineers, construction workers, bartenders, bell-hops, cab drivers, kingpins, pied pipers, window shoppers, guys in turtlenecks, guys in dickies, guys with buzz cuts on top and long in the back, pyros, nymphos, hobos, psychos, sycophants, yahoos, geezers, born-again virgins, butlers, postmodernists, sentries, social workers, presidents and principals and pretentious pundits, pussies, word haters, jackasses, scholars, dragonladies, computer nerds, surfer dudes, jewelers, playwrights, ambassadors, merchants, in-laws, plastic surgeons, neurotics, hand shakers, shakedowners, downplayers, one-uppers, fags, hot air balloonists, bleeders, narcissists, antagonists, mooches, stock brokers, people who carry briefcases, pre-Socratics, phrenologists, collaborators, barmecides, motherfuckers, goat herders, pixie dusters, retards, Buddhists, xenophobes, horticulturalists, fake bakers, hair stylists, cockmongers, native American witch doctors, geishas, mountebanks, jugglers, Shakespeareans, stalkers, butch lesbian badasses, eschatologists, scatologists, stand-up comedians, convenience store porn-browsers, misogynists, bastards, photographers, hebephrenics, haggadists, representatives, deists, simps, spies, Rastifarians, card sharks, contortionists, archers, haberdashers, bird watchers, Big Timers, scriveners, fetishists, fatalists, pec-flexers, tomboys, oafs, addicts, barristers, lion tamers, mindracers, aristocrats, starry-eyed wanderers, gutless prudes, altruists, memorists, insurance salesmen, flâneurs, barbarians, mixers, renovators, movie stars, existentialists, pantheists, hagglers, conjurers, nobodies, disciples, lechers, IRS auditors, stoics, The Spineless, time kippers, The Gullible, fortune-tellers, chiropractors, Brad Pitt lookalikes, stunt women, gunslingers, diamond ring-wearers, pimps in pumps, carpetbag officials, wiggers, telecommunicators, retailers, revenants, editors, mouseketeers, Navy seals, agronomists, cancer patients, goodie-goodies, park rangers, true lovers, Rotarians, genuine eccentrics and wannabe superfreaks, gardeners, postgraduates, pilgrims, neuters and geldings, spongers, hog callers, beer gogglers, secretaries with double-Ds or warts, eyebrow pluckers, wayfarers, bricklayers, hermaphrodites, bottle breakers, bohemians, foragers, midgets, mechanics, village idiots, masseurs, apparatchiks, hangers-on, darkhorses, supreme court justices, egalitarians, trippers, askers, organ donors, organ grinders, coolies, lawyers, joiners, listeners that nod and say "I see," oopsy-daisiites, optimists, somnambulists, astrologists, lecturers, naked laureates, passion-givers, sadomasochists, satanic clowns, chauffeurs, chevaliers, shit kickers, shit shovelers, shitfaces, shitheads, teaheads, dopeheads, cokeheads, dickheads, junkies, scratch golfers, small town tyrants, sociobiologists, sociopaths, social studies substitute teachers, consumers of Product, inspectors, exterminators, ascetics, aspiring slobs, psychoanalysts, surrealists, bantam weight boxers, part-time Christians, marriage counselors, pigeon feeders, skanks, perverts, purists, professional expatriates, production correspondents, prizefighters, neobeatniks, neonazis, hopeless neuromantics, linguists, feltchers, raging librarians, believers in synchronicity, dickless automatons, thinkers, dreamers, folk healers, percussionists, Spandex czars, local yokels, bag ladies, ravers, thing-doers, messiahs, superball sniffers, dirty sock sniffers, bung sniffers, schemers, conspirators, slanderers, solipsists, Sabbatarians, assistant moth wranglers, all-talk-no-walkers, occultists, self-proclaimed subhumans, zooters, undercover cops, goofballs, feckless adolescents brandishing vampiric widow's peaks, jerry-riggers, egocentrics, amputees, thumb suckers, lap dancers, losers, loners, laughers, electric limelighters, grievers, hurters, Olympic sprinters and gymnasts and livers of life, chemists, dissemblers, wiseasses, bankers, geologists, loiterers, dentists, bulimics, Franz Kafka, paranoiacs, fast food drive-thru clerks, lounge lizards, lead singers, hack artists, nice guys, vegans, flagellants, informers, executive decision-makers, aupair girls, daytime skinny-capp drinkers and nighttime guzzlers of vodka martinis straight up with the olive and the essential conical glass, courtesy callers calling every hour on the hour, zoophiles, logophiles, brontologists, podiatrists, friars, auto-monosexualists, cigar-chewing gumshoes, shock therapists, one-by-oners, benefactors and the branded masses, gynecomasts, estrangers, gesticulators, chin strokers, stone throwers, proctologists, psychedelic mushroom divas, abortionist advocates, air traffic controllers, antique collectors and resellers, mean and nasty and wild and crazy packrats, and an invisible man made visible by a suit of human skin standing by himself in a corner blinking into the maelstrom and then scanning the whitewalls of the room, just one more time, for doors that are not there.

THE MESSAGE

"While curious, this tale didn't seem to accomplish anything particular."
—Rejection letter from the editors of *Indigenous Fiction*

1

An envelope was in my mailbox. I removed it, looked at it. Read it.

My home address in neat cursive handwriting. A return address in the same handwriting, but no name . . .

I carried the envelope through a door. I removed a butterfly knife from a drawer, twisted out the blade, opened the envelope, closed the knife and put it away. Inside the envelope was a single slip of paper that I carefully unfolded with one hand as with the other hand I crumpled up the envelope into a tight ball and deposited it in the nearest trash receptacle. No date on the slip of paper, no name or address, no Dear, no Sincerely or Cordially. Only a message. It was in the very middle of the paper and had been typed there in bold print. It read:

I have a message for you.

I blinked . . . Then I threw the message away and started wondering if I should eat a snack, take a power nap, or do some push-ups. Should I do one of these things, or all of them, or just two of them? And if I choose to do two or all of them, in what order should I proceed?

2

An envelope was in my mailbox. I removed it, turned it over a few times in my hands. Read it.

My home address in neat cursive handwriting. A return address in the same handwriting, but no name. On the stamp was a picture of Elvis, the fat one. Stamped on the stamp was the date and the name of the city I lived in. There was nothing else.

I carried the envelope through a door. I removed a butterfly knife from a drawer, twisted out the blade, opened the envelope, closed the knife and put it away. Inside the envelope was a single slip of paper that I carefully unfolded with one hand as with the other hand I crumpled up the envelope into a tight ball and deposited it in the nearest trash receptacle. No date on the slip of paper, no name or address, no Dear, no Sincerely or Cordially. Only a message. It was in the very middle of the paper and had been typed there in bold print. It read:

I have a message for you.

I stared plain-faced at the message for half a minute, reading it over and over . . . Then I placed the message on a desk and walked into a kitchen. I opened and stared into a refrigerator . . . ate a few pieces of ersatz crab meat and washed the snack down with a small glass of orange juice . . . dabbed the corners of my mouth with a paper towel, walked back to the desk, picked up the message and read it once more before crumpling it up and throwing it away.

3

An envelope was in my mailbox. I saw it there, and closed my mailbox. Then I opened it back up and removed the envelope and read it and carried it through a door, squinting at the stamp, a head shot of James Dean, who was smiling like a Howdy Doody ventriloquist doll. "Or *is* that Howdy Doody?" I muttered to myself.

Without opening it, I placed the envelope on a desk and frowned at the return address. Was it familiar?

As familiar as it was the last two times I saw it.

I used a butterfly knife to open the envelope which I balled up tightly and threw in the nearest trash receptacle after I finished opening and closing and returning the knife to the drawer I removed it from and as I did this I unfolded the slip of paper I had removed from inside the envelope with my eyes closed and I held the paper in front of my closed eyes for a ten count. Then I opened my eyes.

I have a message for you.

After reading the message a few times, I turned the slip of paper over. Nothing there. I held the paper up to a light source, still focusing on its backside, and read the message that way. It didn't make sense; most of the letters were backwards. So I removed a pen from a chalice in which there were a number of pens of numerous colors and kinds and on a separate sheet of paper wrote the message down backwards, with the letters forwards, and with the period at the end of it, or rather, at the beginning of it. I read the message aloud.

uoy rof egassem a evah I.

I read the message aloud again, this time in a different accent, a British one. Then I tried on a French, a German, a Slavic, a Mandarin Chinese accent. Then I wrote the message down on a computer screen and began manipulating the period, placing it after the word **rof** first, then in the middle of **egassem**, between the **a** and the first **s**. Then I started manipulating letters, trying to form legible or nearly legible words, particularly out of **egassem**, which had the most potential, which was the heart of the message syntactically and semantically, but which refused to be decoded into anything but the word **message** . . . unless, of course, I considered it phonetically.

"He gassed 'em?" I said. I fingered my chin. "He gassed . . . *me?*" I fingered my chin some more.

Then threw the slip of paper in the nearest trash receptacle.

4

An envelope was in my mailbox. I yelped.

Everything was the same as before except for the stamp, a tiny bushel of raspberries with leaves that resembled poison ivy . . . I dashed through a door, slammed and locked it behind me, ripped opened the envelop with my fingers and speed-read the message inside of it.

I have a message for you.

I yelped again. Then, sighing, I sat down at a desk. I rubbed my eyes with my knuckles until my eyes were red-rimmed and veiny and leaking, so I removed a little bottle of eye drops from a drawer and applied three drops in each eye, waited for my eyes to feel better, returned the eye drops to the drawer and turned to the computer keyboard on the desktop, which I stared at for several minutes before attacking it with my fingers and typing my own message and printing it out. It read:

Fine. What is the message?

After removing the slip of paper with my message on it from a printer tray, I folded it up and slipped it into an envelope. On the front of the envelope I wrote in neat cursive handwriting the nameless return address I had come to know by rote, and above it, in big angry letters, I wrote the word:

YOU

I licked and sealed the envelope. I put a stamp on it. On the stamp was an anteater, with a long sniffing trunk, apparently looking around for some ants.

I deposited the envelope in my mailbox and threw up its red metal flag. Then I folded my arms across my chest and began tapping my foot against the earth.

5

An envelope was in my mailbox. An envelope! I removed it, zipped through a door. After I read the message I sat down at a desk and typed and printed out my own message and folded it and sealed it and sent it off. I waited. I looked in my mailbox. An envelope there. I grabbed it and on the other side of a door opened and read it . . . wrote and sent a message back . . . waited . . . read another message, sent another message, waited . . . found, read, wrote, sent, waited, waited. The correspondence persisted for weeks. Finally I got tired and decided to take a shower and a nap, a long one. When I woke I heated up some water and made a cup of Nescafé, savoring the bitter, alive smell.

On a couch I sipped my coffee and reflected on the correspondence, trying not to think about my mailbox, which, as my nap had lasted for days, I had not visited in days. Still, even now I didn't want to go look inside my mailbox. And I wouldn't. Not for a while, at least. Not until I had finished my coffee, at least . . .

The correspondence went something like this, the first message being the one I received after I sent my first message:

I don't understand.

What don't you understand?

Your message.

How is it possible to not understand my message? I believe
my message was fairly clear.

You should not believe in things.

Well, I do believe in things.

That much is clear.

Unlike my message, evidently.

Evidently.

Fine, I retract my message. Pretend you never received it.

I'm afraid I can't do that.

Why?

I'm allergic to pretending. If I pretend to do anything I'll break out in hives and pass out.

That's a lie.

You have the right to call it a lie. Yes, you have that right.

I know I do. I don't need you to tell me what my rights are.

Of course you don't.

This is getting us nowhere.

Nowhere is as fine a place as any to be.

You know what I mean.

Do I?

Yes, you do.

How do you know if I know what you mean?

Look, knock it off. I want to talk about your message. Okay?

Okay. If that's what you want.

It's what I want. Now, in regards to your original message and my original response to it, allow me to rephrase myself.

You can rephrase yourself, or you can not rephrase yourself. It makes no difference to me.

Don't be a snot.

I'm not being a snot.

Yes you are.

You calling me a snot doesn't make me a snot.

Are you going to allow me to rephrase myself or not?

What did I say?

I forgot.

I said go ahead and rephrase yourself. Or don't. Who cares?

If I don't rephrase myself, are you going to continue sending
me your original message?

Yes. No. I don't know.

What kind of answer is that?

No kind. Answers are answers.

Bull.

Bull yourself.

This is idiotic. I'm going to rephrase myself.

As I said, do whatever you want.

I'm going to. You sent me a message, the same message, four times. It read: I have a message for you. Now if this message of yours can be taken at face value, and I think it can, it seems to me that you have a message for me, in addition to the message alerting me to the fact that you have a message for me. In other words, I will be expecting to receive a message from you in the future that semantically, morphologically, syntactically and phonetically reads differently, if only slightly, than your original message, the one I received from you, once again, four times in the past, in a seeming attempt to drive home your point, which has not only been driven home, but up my ass. So. You say you have a message for me. What is the message?

Ah.

Ah what? What do you mean, Ah?

I mean I understand you now.

Really?

Yes, really.

And?

The message is just that.

Just what? Just what is the message?

6

Three cups of Nescafé later . . . I was outside staring at my mailbox, my caffeine-ridden face twitching like an insect. I reached out to open it, second guessed myself. Second-guessed myself three more times and opened the mailbox.

Inside was an envelope. The stamp . . .

. . . slunk through a door . . .

. . . In a bathroom I used my teeth to open the envelope and spit the torn-off end in the nearest trash receptacle. I was sitting on a toilet. I waited a little before pulling out the envelope's contents. Then I stopped waiting . . . Inside the envelope was a slip of paper. Following a brief pause, during which I groaned in relief, I opened it.

There was a message on the slip of paper. It read:

I have a message for you.

THE WALLS

A flock of angry Japanese beetles was all over me. I looked down, expecting to see my naked flesh. But no. The insects' metallic green hides, twitching in consternation, covered me from head to toe, like armor.

Keeping my cool, I began to shed my armor, but the beetles were totally uncompromising, and I ended up losing my cool after all, squawking and clawing at myself as if I might have been on fire. When I had finally gotten them all off of me, they came for me again, leaping into the air all at once. Their rainbow wings droned like hedge cutters.

I opened the door. Hurled myself through it, slammed it. "Ah," I said.

Then I noticed the walls.

They were wearing corduroy suits. Like me, the ceiling and the floor of the room was white and naked; but the walls were all dressed up. All dressed up! In a frenzy I began stripping the walls bare, leaping all over the place and clawing at the suits and tearing them free, and making a big pile of them in the middle of the room. At first I was inspired; I was certain that my efforts were worthwhile and all would turn out well. But I soon realized that the walls, as I quickly undressed them, were just as quickly dressing themselves back up again, opening up their mouths and spitting brand new corduroy suits all over their bodies.

Enraged, I threatened the walls, told them I would knock them down with my bare hands. "I'll get a hammer, a wrecking ball if I have to!" I added. The walls just laughed, though, and started spitting out nicer, more expensive suits. And when, in an attempt to make the best out of things, I tried to put one of the suits on, it went up in a puff of sparks and smoke, burning all the hair off my flesh . . .

It was not long before I was back outside, my feet together, my head thrown back and my arms outstretched. Now I invited the Japanese beetles to consume me . . . only, now they were dead. And most of their hollow, ashen shells had been taken away by the wind.

PUNCH LINE

"And when that damned alien stuck it in my face and shook the dark thing," explains Picadilly Bruce, wild-eyed and gesticulating, "I nearly took a big old yuk in these pants right here!" He points at the pants and the pants, shivering, turn and sprint off stage, tripping twice along the way. Picadilly Bruce's cackle echoes in the amphitheater. Then . . . silence. Thousands of matte black sunglasses stare into the silence as ushers puffing on fat No. 2 Montichristo cigars flow up and down the aisles. The ushers' flashlights emit thin red beams that fall on one crotch after another; their index fingers tap eagerly on the triggers of the handguns dangling from their chastity belts. When the clown lopes out onto the stage—*flip-flap* go his long flat shoes—the flashlights are clumsily discarded and these handguns are unholstered, readied and aimed. The clown howls in melodramatic fear, sideswipes Picadilly Bruce and sends him spinning, then back flips into the orchestra pit with a crash of brass, percussion and woodwinds. Hail of bullets, the rhythmic pounding of kettle drums. Picadilly Bruce on his back . . . bleeding? No, unscathed. He kips erect, dizzy but raging, hawks up a mouthful of phlegm and spits it at the usher nearest the stage. The usher goes up in a fountain of flesh and genitals. The audience roars. Horrified, the live ushers drop their pieces. They masticate and swallow their smoking cigars and make for the enticing, brightly lit emergency exits, vomiting black ash. Picadilly Bruce grins a rictus grin: he knows the exits are all booby trapped, courtesy of the clown, who now toots on a dented french horn. More roaring as the exit doors clank open and the great white breasts muscle their way in. The nipples of the breasts are steel-toothed mouths that chomp and in no time at all every last usher is mutilated and devoured. Grunts, belches, smell of stale milk. The breasts retire, last ones out slam shut the doors. The audience leaps to its feet and, skulls shaking in awe, begins to clap. Picadilly Bruce shushes them with an absolutely expressionless expression. Embarrassed, everybody takes their seats. Some remove their sunglasses and with handkerchiefs make the steamy, sweat-soaked lenses shine, while others merely clear their throats and cough, or adjust bow ties. Picadilly Bruce nods. He raises a finger and dashes off stage. In his absence the clown crouches and jumps up out of the orchestra pit, suspends himself in mid air, rips down frilled boxer briefs and moons the crowd (his ass is hairy and acne-slickered). Then he allows himself to fall, onto his feet, behind a podium. He taps a baton against the metal plate of his bald white head and maestros the orchestra through the beginnings of Pachelbel's Canon in D. When Picadilly Bruce returns the clown silences the orchestra with a sharp cutting motion across the throat, accidentally opening himself up and spurting, and his body jerks and jerks and jerks before coming to rest and in slow-motion toppling over into the barrel of a tuba with a bloody, awkward blurt. Picadilly Bruce blinks at the spectacle. Then, the pants struggling in his firm grasp, he turns to the audience and reiterates the punch line: "I'm telling you now—I almost took a big old yuk in these here pants!" He holds them up, presenting them. The pants gasp and suffocate from the pressure of so many widening eyes. They go limp as a corpse in a noose and now the audience cheers, gets to their feet again, claps till their palms bleed. Picadilly Bruce grants them the pleasure this time, takes a garish bow and, once the curtain falls, slips the pants on, one leg at a time, concealing his greedy nakedness.

CIRCUS

After the cashier gives me my change, we proceed through a rusty turnstile and into the tent. Inside the circus roars. Swinging acrobats, clowns on stilts and in Volkswagens, ferocious demon-faced lions, men in tuxedos and handlebar mustaches, trumpeting elephants and wandering freaks of all shapes and deformities are just a few of the many curios that entertain the onlookers, including Kieri and I. But we get bored quickly. We go and sit down on a pile of bricks that have been smashed and disseminated by the telekinetic frown of an Egyptian mystic that, ironically, had had his face surgically removed and so had no real brow with which to frown. Kieri, who I have positioned on my lap, pulls my ear to her mouth and says something about the mystic's peculiar feat, but I can't hear her very well over the insect hum of all the circus-goers, and at any rate the mystic has disappeared behind a velvet curtain. So I kiss her, and she kisses me back, and soon our tongues are one slippery thing. I slide my hand down her neck and squeeze one of her breasts, then move on to her abdomen and finally her crotch. She coos like a bird and cums. Satisfied, I maneuver her off my lap, rise and ask if she wants anything. She thinks about it for a while, shrugs and says, "I guess not." "Fine, then." I bend over and give her a peck on the cheek and weave my way over to a snack bar. I wait in line. "Sausage dog, please, with sour kraut all over it." "Oui, mon frere! Maintenant!" ejaculates a pale boy with a dead asp wrapped around his head in a turban. He quickly processes the order and I pay, and he gives me my food. "Voila!" he screams. I head over to a condiment table to get some more sour kraut, along with some ketchup and mustard and relish.

The table is crowded but I muscle my way in and out without too much trouble, and soon enough I have returned to Kieri—who, I find, is engaged; that is, she's sitting on somebody else's lap now. This somebody else is a shirtless mesomorph with short-cropped, pumpkin-orange hair. He strokes Kieri's shapely thighs and calves and she in turn strokes his smooth chin; now and again she loses her nose and lips in the curly bright locks of his chest. I stare pointedly at them and take another bite of my sausage dog, chewing on it with a loud, open mouth. They don't acknowledge me. Do they even see me? I take a step closer, tilt back my head and widen my eyes. The mesomorph, pinching the back of Kieri's neck so that she can't turn her head around, looks up at me and with a twitch of his rosebud lips motions me away. I stuff the rest of my sausage dog in my mouth, swallow it in one gulp. Eyeing the mesomorph, I huff and shake my head. He twitches his lips again. I loom there for a moment longer, flexing my jaw . . . Then I leave. Head down, I weave my way through the chinks and crevices of the buzzing masses, take a wrong turn and find myself in a dank elephant shithouse pinching my nose, get out of there, get lost again, this time in somebody's dressing room, as much a maze as everywhere else in this place. Convinced there is no way out, I collapse into a not uncomfortable Naugahyde chair and stare at myself in a dusty, dimly lit mirror. And minutes, possibly hours later—there he is, behind me. "Ah ha!" I exclaim. I spring to my feet and face him, then pause, smacking my lips. "Say, do you know how to get out of here? I've been trying to get out, you see. My girlfriend . . . well, do you think you can give me a hand?" "Yes. I think I can," rasps the naked Egyptian mystic through a mouth that doesn't exist. Then he grabs hold of his hideously erect nipples and yanks back, opening himself up—sound of tearing Velcro—and flashing me, exposing me to his rib cage and the shiny wiggling organs lodged behind the bone.

"You fool!" I laugh. "How do you expect me to negotiate that?" But the mystic, petting his moth-eaten intestines with a finger, can only nod at me in dark, faceless understanding.

THE PROFESSORS

The professors do everything together. They teach courses together. They write essays together. They speedwalk down hallways together. They perform absent-minded feats together. They drink strong coffee and stronger Rob Roys together. They go home together, they sleep together.

And, of course, they urinate together.

"This pissoir has manure all over it!" exclaimed one of the professors after they had all crowded inside and shut and locked the door behind them. "All over the walls, all over the ceiling, all over the floor, all over the hole in which we are presumably supposed to urinate—indeed, gentlemen, there is manure everywhere!"

"Don't be so sure," said another one of the professors and smiled the smile that all professors smile when they smile, with one lip corner all the way up and the other all the way down. "This could be a trick."

Another professor raised an eyebrow and said, "An attractive contention, sir. After all, the so-called manure that, our colleague argues, is all over 'everything', as it were, may not be manure at all, but merely some other substance *disguised* as manure. For all we know, the inside of this pissoir is cloaked from head to toe in a perfectly harmless, perfectly scentless substance—Play Dough, in all likelihood—that has been dyed the color of manure and sprayed with a spray can of manure-scented potpourri!"

"I don't buy it, I don't buy it," huffed another professor, shaking his head. "First of all, Play Dough is most definitely not scentless, it has a distinct smell that, personally, I find attractive and repellant at one and the same time. Second, it is not perfectly harmless: numerous children have, since its introduction into the consumer market, swallowed and choked to death on Play Dough; thus it has proved harmful. Third, of the many colors that Play Dough is available in, the color of manure (*brown*, it's called) is one of them and so there would be no point in the party responsible for this atrocity purchasing yellow or red or blue Play Dough and then dying it brown when Play Dough is available for purchase *in* brown. Fourth, potpourri is a mixture of flour petals, not one of which, even when it rots, smells anything like manure."

"Here here," chirped at least three professors.

Another professor chirped, "I disagree. It is my belief that rotten flower petals and manure smell very much alike, very much alike indeed. In addition—and here I am addressing those of us who have curiously referred to this place as a pissoir—this is not a pissoir. A pissoir is a public urinal located in the streets of some European countries that is not enclosed by walls or a ceiling. Have you gentlemen forgotten about our recent venture to Roma? Evidently so. No, this is not a pissoir. This is a port-a-john. Moreover, if what is on the walls, ceiling, floor and hole of this port-a-john is in fact manure, it would necessitate that a cow, not a human, come in here and excrete all over the place. I don't know about you gentlemen, but no cow I have ever laid eyes on could possibly squeeze its great bulk into such a small area, let alone excrete with such . . . dynamism."

At this point the professors began speaking all at once, a phenomenon that never ceased to annoy both the professors and anybody that might have been listening to them, especially when they were teaching, since all that could be heard was the sound of television static turned on full blast. But one by one the professors forced themselves to silence themselves, albeit to do so was always a trying affair. Why should I silence myself, this or that professor would ask himself, when all of my colleagues continue to produce the very antipode of silence? Still, eventually there were only a few professors speaking, and then there were none. Then another, tamer dialogue began.

"It smells!"

"Yes, that is what it does. Smells."

"A fine mess we're in!"

"Yes, a fine mess. We're packed in here like sardines and this smell, if we endure it much longer, will destroy us."

"No it won't. You're being histrionic now. In truth, we could stay in here and endure this smell for centuries and centuries, if food and drink was made available to us on a regular basis, as well as geriatric treatments."

A series of giggles and clucks here. Then this response: "I'm sorry, but that is nothing less than a ridiculous thing to say. For we have no food and drink and nobody is going to bring us any, unless one of us has planned in advance for this little misadventure, unless one of us has informed an outsider that at such and such a time, in such a such a place, there is such and such a port-a-john, and so forth. And geriatric treatments, pills or injections or implants or suppositories that have the capacity to prolong life for centuries on end . . . well, that is the stuff of science fiction literature—the study of which, incidentally, is a waste of any serious academic's time, as we all know. Now then. We're in a predicament here. Let's see if we can't think our way out it rationally, shall we?"

"There is no way out."

"No way out?" The professor that spoke these words blinked, hard, then harder, as if blinking hard and then harder would erase the words "no way out" from existence, or in any case from his own subjectivity. It didn't. "Come now, gentlemen. There must be a way out. There is *always* a way out."

"I disagree. I think there are cases, not necessarily this one, but possibly this one, that cannot be negotiated. Cases that bind one by the wrists and ankles and refuse to let one go home, no matter what one does."

"For absurdists, perhaps. For those who like Sisyphus are doomed to roll the boulder up the hill only to have it fall back upon him time and again, forever and ever, I admit, there is no way out. But we are not Sisyphus. We are professors! And we must start acting like professors! Otherwise we will die in here. Make no mistake about it: this smell, this sight, whatever it is, whatever its origin—it *will* destroy us."

"This professor is correct. The possibility that we will be destroyed is a very real one."

"I have no idea, no idea at all what we should do."

"I, too, have no idea. I'm at a loss. For the first time since I received my tenure, I'm at a loss."

The professor that had attempted to blink away the words "no way out" attempted to blink away the words "at a loss," this time with a machine gun fusillade of blinks that proved as ineffectual as any method of blinking. So he said, "A loss? A loss! It's one thing to have no idea, even no idea at all. But it's quite another thing to be at a loss. A professor at a loss? Nonsense!"

"It is not nonsense, sir. It is the truth."

"The truth? The truth! Why, as I understand it, and as I formerly presupposed all of us professors understood it, the only existing truth is that truth does not exist. Thus your claim that my claim is fallacious renders my claim brazenly accurate. In other words, when you say, 'It is not nonsense, sir, it is the truth,' you are steeping yourself in contradiction. For if truth is the signature of the predominance of falsehood, why, what you say is *not* nonsense is *absolute* nonsense—is so nonsensical that I can barely contain myself!"

"Please, gentlemen, please. Let's not lose our wits. Our wits are all we have going for us right now."

"Wits are for real estate salesmen. We are not real estate salesmen. We are professors!"

"I do not need to be told what we are and what we are not—not once, certainly not twice. What we are and are not is by all means perfectly clear to me. What is *not* perfectly clear to me is how we are supposed to liberate ourselves from this— situation! What, pray tell, will function as our agency?"

"I have a suggestion."

There was a pause. The pause was followed by another pause, during which all of the professors save the one that had said "I have a suggestion" glanced back and forth at one another in dumbfounded hysteria. Then one of them said, "What did this professor say?"

"I have a suggestion," repeated the professor. "That is what I said."

"Did this professor just say he had a suggestion?"

"I believe he did."

"I believe he did as well."

"As do I."

"And I."

"The 'I's have it!" said a professor and raised a finger in the air. The finger crumpled against the ceiling of the port-a-john and was mired. "Disgusting!" spat the professor. He attacked the finger with a surge of dubious sniffs as another professor spat, "A suggestion? A professor claims to have a suggestion and fails to articulate that suggestion immediately after stating that he has it in his possession? Nonsense!"

Another professor said, "It *is* nonsense; there is no two ways about it. But perhaps this instance of nonsense would not have manifested itself in the absence of our present circumstance. I'm willing to give my distinguished colleague the benefit of the doubt and hear him out. Am I alone in this matter?"

"You are not alone!!!" harmonized the professors.

"Fine, then. We will hear him out. What is the suggestion, sir?"

The professor that had claimed to have a suggestion cleared his throat before speaking. He was a new professor—his Ph.D. had been acquired not even a year ago and it would be at least five years before he received tenure, this assuming he published enough critical essays in enough reputable scholarly journals in that time—and he always cleared his throat before speaking, unlike his colleagues, the youngest of which stopped clearing his throat before he spoke over a decade ago. "My suggestions is this," said the professor. "We could urinate."

Dead, appaling silence. Then:

"We could . . . *what*?"

"What could we do?"

"What?"

"Excuse me?"

"We could do *what*?"

"Say again?"

"What's that now?"

"What?"

"What?"

"What? What could—"

"We could urinate!" the professor yelled. Realizing the others continued to lack comprehension, he added, "We could all unzip our pants, take out our penises, urinate, put away our penises, zip up our pants, unlock and open the door of the pissoir—pardon me, the port-a-john—and exit the port-a-john. That way, we won't die in here. And after all, that's why we came in here. To urinate."

Again the suggestion, despite that it had been made clear, was met with dead, appalling silence. The silence persisted for a number of minutes before being broken by an eruption of thunderous, long-winded laughter that culminated in all of the professors, including the one that had made the suggestion, who eventually joined in the laughter for fear of being the only one not laughing, passing out all over themselves . . . and then regaining consciousness, and going about their business.

THE EYEBALLS

There is nothing out of the ordinary about Dr. Thunderlove's eyeballs in themselves. They are fine-looking eyeballs, white as a pair of freshly brushed teeth with only a hint of red lightning here and there, and with sea blue irises that are radiant enough to make you double-take the good doctor, but not so radiant that, when you do double-take him, you fail to realize that his irises are the real thing and not the product of tinted contact lenses. Additionally, the eyeballs are perfectly round, not egg-shaped like, say, a pair of myopic eyeballs. As far as eyeballs go, these things are the best things going. The only problem with them—and this is no fault of the eyeballs themselves—is that they are on the outside of Dr. Thunderlove's head.

"Mother was a giant lobster," he often jokes with his patients.

Dr. Thunderlove is a pediatrician, however, and it's a rare occasion that a patient leaves his office with dry cheeks and without more than enough psychological baggage for at least a month's worth of nightmares. Who can blame them? Here is a man with two big round eyeballs perched on the ends of a pair of slick green-grey stalks that each stretch half a foot or so out of his eye sockets; and if a patient gets near enough to one of these eye sockets—when the doctor is probing the nostrils, for instance—the frontal lobe of his brain becomes screamingly visible. It is very ugly-looking, this brain. It smells funny, too.

"That?" he once said to a little girl that had seen the brain and was hyperventilating for the sixth time that visit. "That's nothing. That's just a big old ball of bubble gum. Whenever I'm done chewing a piece, I stick it in my head. Lot better than tossing it on the ground for somebody to step on, don't you think? Remember: nobody likes a litterbug."

Naturally, living with your eyeballs on the outside of your head can be a real drag and, for some people, too much of a drag to bear; no matter how many support groups they go to, no matter how many self-help kits they buy, no matter how drunk and stoned they get, no matter how many times a day they go to church—some people just can't cope. Dr. Thunderlove, on the contrary, is a very well-adjusted individual. Just by looking at him you can tell he doesn't spend an inordinate amount of time thinking about how his eyes are sticking out of his fleshy, ruddy-cheeked face like a couple of golf balls on moldy celery sticks, and he certainly doesn't seem insecure about it. However, there is one thing that really bothers him about his idiosyncrasy, and that is the constant wetting and rewetting of the idiosyncracy. All day long there is a nurse sitting on top of his shoulders, moistening his eyeballs with a saline dropper every fifteen seconds (or less, depending on if the windows in his office are open and a breeze is blowing), and whereas this nurse is a lightweight midget and not much of a strain on Dr. Thunderlove's shoulders, it's still a tedious process—especially when he goes home and has to apply the saline solution himself, since his wife refuses to do it, not because her husband's eyeballs freak her out, but because she is absolutely in love with herself and can't be bothered with anybody except herself. In fact, not once during their four years of marriage, or during their dating years, had she so much as mentioned the eyeballs, which the doctor believed she truly didn't see, not ever, as all of her attention, at all times of the day and night, is focused on her own well-being.

"I should've married an ugly person," Dr. Thunderlove once told Dr. Aquiline, the plastic surgeon with whom he shares his office. "I got too much love to dish out to be ignored by her,

Ak. Just say my name out loud and you'll know it's the truth!"

"I know it, I know it," said Dr. Aquiline and offered to fix him up, free of charge. He refused. Dr. Thunderlove is greatly saddened by his wife's apathy towards him, but not *that* saddened. And even if he was sad enough to get an eye job for her, she probably wouldn't even notice; she has yet to notice that his eyeballs are on the outside of his head, why should she notice if they were suddenly on the inside? No, the doctor is not willing to put himself under the knife for that awful woman, or anybody for that matter. Even his patients. Granted, he hardly enjoys the shrieks, the backwards cat leaps, the open-mouthed terror he evokes every time he walks into an examining room, nor does he enjoy the bawling and the sniffling and the mom-calling that follows. But the way Dr. Thunderlove sees it, life is full of hair-raising things and it's best if children get used to it here at the beginning of life, so they'll be better prepared for it later on.

"If you can't handle my eyeballs right now," Dr. Thunderlove often says to his patients, especially the ones who can't stop soiling themselves, "when you grow up—how do you expect to handle the real world?"

THE NOSE

"I am led, therefore, to regard the function of the mirror-stage as a particular case of the function of the *imago*, which is to establish a relation between the organism and its reality."

— Jacques Lacan, "The mirror stage as formative of the function of the I as revealed in psychoanalytic experience"

After finishing up with his cheeks, chin and neck, the thing-doer examined his nose. It was a very hairy nose, despite the young age of the thing-doer, and he had been putting off shaving it for many hours. Every time he shaved it, of course, the hair grew back twice as thick, twice as fast, and it was so thick and fast-growing now that, if he shaved it again . . .

But the nose hair was out of control; it had to be taken care of, no matter the consequences. He could not worry about the future of the condition of his nose at this point. "Concentrate on the present," he told his reflection in the mirror. "The present is all that exists anyway. The past, the future, I can't touch these things with my fingertips." Granted, by lunchtime his nose hair might be growing so fast that he would be able to see it go (he could almost see it go now, if he concentrated), and no doubt after lunch, while he took his daily nap, it would grow into his nostrils and mouth and suffocate him. But nap time was a long way off. For now, for the next hour or so at least, his nose would be, while far from being smooth as a baby's bottom, smooth enough for life.

The thing-doer lifted the blade to the upper bridge of his nose and placed it there. He licked his lips. Taking a deep breath, he prepared himself for the long, slow swipes that would do the job . . .

"Stop!" I shouted, unable to contain myself any longer, and pointed at my own nose, the nose right in front of his face. Which was not a nose at all, but a genital.

THE MOUTHS

My ear holes had turned into mouths. The mouths had teeth and tongues and I could still hear out of them, but I could also taste and talk with them, too—or rather, they could taste and talk, for I had no control over them, had no idea what they might say or lick next, which was a little frustrating, but I got used to it. I get used to everything.

"How is it that you're able to do that, my man?" implored an attorney and flicked another hors d'oeuvre into his mouth. I was standing in the middle of a cocktail party and the attorney was talking to the mouth in my right ear. The mouth in my left ear was talking to a prostitute that was, every so often, goosed by a passing gigolo—the cocktail party consisted of nothing more than attorneys, prostitutes and gigolos (and me and my mouths of course)—and had somehow coerced her into paying it fifty dollars if she would lay down and let the mouth perform oral sex on her.

After slipping a crinkled up fifty dollar bill in my back pocket, she lay down.

"If I could only get this old head to lean over now," said the mouth in my left ear to me, out of the corner of its mouth as it were, but I wasn't about to oblige it. After all, the mouth in my right ear was talking to somebody, and so was I, with my regular mouth. My interlocutor was perhaps the most attractive female attorney at the party, and that was nice—so nice that I wasn't upset by her insistence on monopolizing the conversation. I imagined the prospect of a silence, however slight, developing between us frightened her, and prompted her to yabber on about all of her selfless cats and about the gigolo who kept evil-eyeing her and about her most recent, most interesting case. At any rate, there she was, and there was the mouth in my right ear, which was now being fed spoonfuls of caviar and bacon-wrapped shrimps by its martini-logged interlocutor. So I was not about to indulge the mouth in my left ear. My resolve was made firmer by the fact that this mouth had stuck out its long, heavy tongue in an attempt to weight me down to the floor, where the prostitute was patiently waiting for it.

"It won't work," I whispered, out of the corner of my regular mouth now, and tightened up the cords in my neck. "Stop it, you."

The mouth in my left ear kept at it for a while longer, but soon the prostitute grew weary; after reaching up into my pocket and taking her money back, she turned over onto her belly and scuttled away on her elbows. The mouth, realizing it had been defeated, sucked in its tongue.

"You bastard," it said to me . . . and produced a farting noise. It was an expert ventriloquist and made it sound like the farting noise had hailed from my ass. Except for the attorney in front of me, who went on gabbing, everybody sucked in their cheeks and moved one step away.

I made a face and said, "Pardon *me,*" interrupting the attorney. She had been discussing a recent John Grisham novel, something about how the protagonist was schizoid effective and couldn't be trusted. "Would you pardon me for a moment?" Her face froze and she suffered five seconds of silence. This clearly got the best of her, for two seconds after that she was nervously pushing her way towards the bathroom.

Out of the corner of the left side of my mouth I intoned, "You're the bastard. Why can't you act like a normal mouth? Well, maybe not like a normal mouth, maybe not like that. But like something with a little class. What's your problem anyway? You're no good. Given the opportunity, I bet you'd eat me up. Me, and everything else you could get your grubby teeth on."

"Agreed!" said the mouth in my right ear, who had been eavesdropping, and who was all by itself now, its interlocutor having passed out drunk.

"Maybe you and I," I said out of the right corner of my regular mouth to the mouth in my right ear, but loud enough so that the mouth in my left hear could hear me, "should eat up *this one*." With my thumb I motioned at the mouth in my left ear, who I expected to holler at us—so easy to get a rise out of that one, especially when we ganged up on it—but instead it just muttered a few harmless obscenities. Still, the mouth in my right ear and I got a kick out of it and had a good laugh. In fact, we laughed all the way out of the cocktail party, taming ourselves only to sweet talk a couple of prostitutes into following us out the exit doors.

THE CHIN

Guitar Man was walking down the street with Secret Agent Woman at lunchtime and Secret Agent Woman was talking about what they should do, go get some food, or go into an alley and fornicate. Guitar Man wasn't hungry or horny, though; right now he just wanted to play his guitar. The guitar was made of flesh, bone and donkey hair. It was growing out of his rib cage and when he opened his mouth to ask Secret Agent Woman, "Can I go play my guitar?" his chin turned into a perch. A wet golden brown perch that flapped its down-pointed tail and flexed all of its shiny, spiny fins.

"Whoa," said Secret Agent Woman, coming to a sharp halt. Her neck cracked when she cocked her head.

Guitar man pushed out his fish-chin a little and peered down past his nose and lips. "What's going on here?" he said. "Who did this to me? You? I demand to know. I demand to know immediately."

Secret Agent Woman, clearly disgusted, didn't answer. Guitar Man wondered if she was disgusted by the accusation that she was in some way responsible for the fish-chin or by the fish-chin itself. He was about to ask her when she grabbed hold of a passerby, Bodybuilder Man, by his bronze, cleanly shaven pectoral muscles and dragged him kicking and screaming into the closest alley—to fornicate with him, no doubt. Guitar Man watched them go. So did some other passersby. But most passersby found Guitar Man's newfangled eccentricity more interesting than his girlfriend's nymphomania, and they approached him . . .

The first person to approach Guitar Man was Dead Soul

Woman. Dead Soul Woman didn't have any bones or organs or muscles inside of her skin. All she had in there was a slimy, cruddy soul corpse that, like most human-sized corpses, felt much heavier dead than when it was alive, and the stress it exerted on her body and mind insured that she was always in a bad mood . . . except when she was eating key lime pie. The taste of key lime pie allowed her both to forget about her burden and to cease to feel it inside of her, and if Dead Soul Woman could have it her way, she would spoon it into her open mouth all day and night, nonstop. Unfortunately key lime pie had recently been put on the endangered species list and in a week's time jumped from $1.09 a slice to $2,500 a slice, a price that Dead Soul Woman's budget couldn't accommodate; of course, this accentuated the badness of her mood. So Dead Soul Woman, swearing underneath her breath, hobbled up to Guitar Man and, motioning at his fish-chin with her own spittle-stained chin, said, "Curious, very curious. It almost makes me want to like you. But I despise you. I despise you as much as a disgusting smell, any disgusting smell will do. And now that I have told you this, let me tell you something else: you are very ugly, even without that bombastic perch on you. *Especially* without that bombastic perch. Clearly you've conjured that perch onto yourself in order to deter passersby like me from noticing you and your unforgivable ugliness. You make me so sick I want to vomit. In fact, I'm going to vomit right now." Dead Soul Woman turned to one side and vomited on a fire hydrant. At the time Canine Man was pissing on it and so both he and the fire hydrant imploded with a high-pitched little screech. "There, you bastard," griped Dead Soul Woman, wiping flecks of every edible thing except key lime pie from her lips. "I hope you're proud of yourself. Are you proud of yourself?"

Guitar Man blinked at her. Moans, grunts, shrieks, taboo words, a torrent of stinking insults seeped out of the alley in which Secret Agent Woman was having her way with Body-builder Man.

"I didn't think so," said Dead Soul Woman. She shook her head in hate and hobbled away, purposely elbowing Guitar Man in the guitar as she brushed past him. Guitar Man wanted to take his own elbow and swing it into her face but he was still too worried about what had happened to him, and why, and who was responsible for it, to actuate himself in any way. Not to mention that, the moment Dead Soul Woman left him, he was approached by another person, Fly Swatter Salesman Man, who exclaimed, "Good day, sir. I hope you'll pardon the intrusion but I was just passin you by when I noticed that your chin just up and changed into a perch and I wanted to tell you a little somethin bout this product of mine which you'll be needin in a quick when that there perch goes stale and the flies come lookin to feel you with their dirtyrotten feelers so let me cut right to the goddamn chase if you don't mind cuz I'm a busy man, no shit." Fly Swatter Salesman Man reached over his shoulder and into a holster strapped to his back. He removed his product as if it might be a sword, brandishing it, then lowering and holding it up in front of his face, which had moved its way to within just a few inches of Guitar Man's face. Guitar Man tried to widen the space between the two faces but the brick wall of the convenience store behind him prohibited it. "It's lightweight," said Fly Swatter Salesman Man, "it's durable, it's reasonably priced, and best of all—it swats! Don't believe me? I'll prove it! Just you watch, boy!"

As Fly Swatter Salesman Man took a step back and began swatting the air between them, huffing and puffing more intensely with each exaggerated swat, Guitar Man lightly thrummed on the donkey haired strings of his guitar. Dead Soul Woman's elbow had knocked the instrument out of tune, but still, the thrumming soothed him, if only for a second or two.

In his periphery Guitar Man saw Secret Agent Woman emerge from the alley with the bloody corpse of Bodybuilder Man. She stuffed it in the gutter. Then she surveyed the passersby, sizing them up and down, and, when she found one that looked sex-worthy, grabbed it. It was *La belle dame sans merci* Woman. She had horns growing out of every orifice, including her pores, and all of the horns were covered in excrement. Secret Agent Woman took *La belle dame sans merci* Woman by the horn growing out of her navel and led her into the alley. Sex sounds ensued.

For a moment Guitar Man lost himself in a mnemonic reverie involving he and Secret Agent Woman and a seemingly impossible sexual position called The Hideous Nirp. The reverie quickly dissolved, however, when Fly Swatter Salesman Man's fly swatter accidentally got too close to Guitar Man's face and swatted it across the nose, cheek, lips and fish-chin. At first he felt nothing but his head turning to one side. Then the pain kicked in and on instinct he cursed. Fly Swatter Salesman Man, also on instinct, ran away.

"I never forget a fuckin asshole!" Guitar Man wanted to shout. But the pain in his face was too great and he had to busy himself with transferring some of the pain elsewhere, namely to his tongue and guitar shaft, which, respectively, he bit and pinched. It worked. And when the pain completely withdrew from his face he took his teeth off his tongue and his fingernails off his guitar shaft, and waited for that pain, now bearable, to go away. It did. Then Cyberpunk Woman, Mafia Man, Neanderthal Man Man and Dystopia Woman approached Guitar Man and without a word beat him up, their collective hunch being that his mutated chin was a screaming act of oneupmanship, no matter who was responsible for it.

"It's not the actuator who must answer for the act,"

Neanderthal Man Man told his companions as they left the crumpled, unconscious heap that was Guitar Man in their dust, "it's the actor himself."

When Guitar Man regained consciousness, he uncrumpled himself and stood up. Twenty or so more passersby approached him, one by one, and made fun of, bad-mouthed, and/or complained about his chin in various and sundry ways. Then, suddenly, Film Noir Man was in front of him, staring at him. Film Noir Man had a film noir face with a film noir hairdo and he was wearing a film noir outfit with film noir shoes and shoe laces. He lived on Film Noir Street and drove a film noir car and smoked film noir cigarettes and dined in film noir restaurants and was by all means the epitome of film noir. Every breath of air he took into his lungs was a film noir breath and he lived his life according to a strict film noir code of laws. That he ironically hated film noir films reduced that code of laws to rubble, of course, but no Film Noir Man is an island.

"I also hate live performances," blurted Film Noir Man in a film noir tone of voice, as if Guitar Man was aware of the irony. "On tv, on stage, in my garage, wherever. Do you want to know why I hate live performances? I'll tell you: I'm always worried the other actors are going to screw up and embarrass me." Film Noir Man raised his hands. In one quick film noir gesture, he pointed all of his fingers, save his pinky fingers, which curled up into such tight circles that they were no longer visible, at Guitar Man's fish-chin. "Sir," he ejaculated, "I am embarrassed!"

Here Guitar Man, once again, out of the corners of his eyes, spotted Secret Agent Woman stealing another passerby into the alley, after disposing of the last passerby she had stolen (and screwed and killed) in the gutter. This time, though, as she ducked into the alley, she gave Guitar Man a glance, but his perception of it was too peripheral to determine whether the glance was laughing at him, or taking pity on him, or being tender, or being malicious, or just being empty. He nearly asked Film Noir Man, who for a moment turned his head to gape and hoot-whistle at Secret Agent Woman (she was very attractive), if he could tell him what the glance was all about, but the expression on Film Noir Man's face looked like an expression that would not only not respond to such a question, it would hiss at and perhaps attack it. So Guitar Man played it safe and kept his mouth shut.

A pigeon passed overhead and shat on Film Noir Man's shoulder. Thinking Vanilla Ice Cream Cone Eater Man had bumped into him, Film Noir Man casually dabbed the shit with his index finger and licked it . . . and exploded, getting Guitar Man's fish-chin all wet with film noir viscera.

Guitar Man removed a handkerchief from his back pocket and began to clean off the fish-chin. It was bruised and inflamed in places from his recent beating, and when he dabbed at it the tail flip-flapped with far less enthusiasm than it originally had, mostly from the beating, but also because the perch was on the verge of drying out . . . and dying? What would happen if the perch died on his face? Would it disappear? If that was the case, Guitar Man would strangle the fish right now so that he could get off the wall he was backed up against and get on with his life. But there was no way to be certain that the perch would disappear if it died. For all he knew, he would spend the rest of his life walking around with a smelly, moldy, fly- and maggot-infested fish corpse hanging from his chin, unless he opted to spend the rest of his life walking around holding a fishbowl of lake water under his chin so that the fish wouldn't die and smell and attract even more attention than it did when it was alive. He would have to get a fish bowl quickly, if that's what he was going to do. But if he went and got a fish bowl and kept his chin alive there would be no way of knowing whether or not, if the chin died, it would go away.

The more he thought about what he should do, or rather, what he should not do, the more depressed Guitar Man became; and the question of how the fish-chin came to be, and who was responsible, enhanced his grief. Even thrumming on his now obscenely out of tune guitar didn't help. Nor did the fact that his girlfriend, who persisted in dragging person after person into and out of the alley, had turned into a kind of serial killer.

"But hasn't she always been a serial killer?" Guitar Man whispered to himself, his memory oddly failing him. "Or are her actions an effect of my metamorphosis?"

"Does it really matter?" said Kafka Man. During Guitar Man's meditation he had backed up against the wall next to him, so that they were just a hair's breadth away from being shoulder to shoulder. Kafka Man gazed out into the thick, fast-moving throng of passersby on the sidewalk as he spoke. "Does it really matter one way or the other what Secret Agent Woman has always been, what she is now, or, for that matter, what she will become?"

Guitar Man didn't turn his head and face Kafka Man—that may or may not be rude—but he did examine him thoroughly out of his eye corners. Kafka Man was slim, well-built and handsome. His ears stuck way out (he might have been able to fly away with those ears) and his steel-blue eyes were animated and shining. He was wearing a three piece suit and bowler hat the same color as his eyes, with a blood-red tie, and the quiet smile on his face was described by both pain and wisdom. There was definitely a very unusual aura of power about him, Guitar Man could see and feel it; but there was also a sense of weakness. An electric shadow, Kafka Man appeared to be luminous and char-broiled at once.

Kafka Man spoke to Guitar Man for five minutes about

random commonplace things and every single word he spoke, despite the commonplace it referred to, was meaningful; not a shallow phrase emerged from his lips. Guitar Man remained silent. He wanted to say something but was afraid of insulting Kafka Man by speaking words that reeked of meaninglessness, and in any case Kafka Man was a wonderful speaker and he was perfectly content just listening to him. That Kafka Man was the first person not to remark on or make fun of his fish-chin made him even more content, albeit a small part of him expected some kind of remark to be made soon.

No such remark was made. For a while Guitar Man wondered if Kafka Man had even noticed his fish-chin . . . until Kafka Man said, "Dreams come along, they come up the river, on a ladder they climb the quayside. One stops, one talks to them, they know so much, only where they come from, that they don't know." He paused. During the pause he dry-heaved, burped and farted a few times. "Pardon me," he said. Then, just as abruptly as he had placed his back against the wall next to Guitar Man, Kafka Man removed his back from the wall, took a step forward, and leapt into the furious stream of passersby.

Guitar Man wanted to follow Kafka Man. And he would follow him. *Now.* But just as he took a step forward, his fish-chin turned into a black hole-chin that sucked his skin (and the clothes and hair on top of the skin) off, and he had to double over to keep his organs from spilling onto his toes . . .

THE COCKTAIL PARTY

I threw myself through the door. I don't know who the door belonged to. Nor did I have a reason for throwing myself through it. Do I have a reason for doing anything? Well, there was the door, and there was my body, and then there was my body flying through the door in a hail of screaming splinters. True, I could have opened the door and walked through it no problem. In fact, there was a little neon sign on it that said: OPEN ME UP AND WALK THROUGH ME. But to do that would have been too easy. I don't like things to be too easy. Anything that is too easy usually comes back to you and bites you in your unsuspecting ass.

The great force with which I threw myself through the door was more than enough to get me airborn and as I was flying through the air I noticed four things:

1. There's nobody in this room I've thrown myself into.
2. This must be like a foyer or something.
3. The wallpaper on the walls is disturbingly unattractive.
4. My face is heading for a welcome mat.

When my face struck the welcome mat, the welcome mat actually said, "Welcome." I passed out. When I woke I said, "Where am I?" I really didn't know. I didn't even know my name. I knew I was a living thing, that's all. I had lost my memory. Then all of a sudden I found my memory, remembered my name and where I was. Or did I? People are losing their memories all the time. Who's to say that the memory I retrieved wasn't somebody else's loss?

No way to tell.

I stood up, looked around. The room I was in was a not-too-small, not-too-large room with no furniture and no windows. Save the ugly wallpaper, the walls had only three things to offer:

1.   A long line of hooks with coats hanging on them.
2.   The door I had thrown myself through, which was no longer a door but a jagged-edged hole.
3.   Another door, diametrically opposite to the door I had thrown myself through, that also had a neon sign on it. This one said: DO NOT OPEN ME UP BY THROW-ING YOURSELF THROUGH ME.

Beneath this second door was the welcome mat my face had landed on and apparently broke: instead of saying "Welcome" now the mat was talking a lot of drunken gibberish—grunting and belching, making car revving sounds, claiming it was the antichrist and so on. I wanted to stomp on and shut it up but I was in too much pain. This is what I looked like:

The pricks sticking out all over me are door splinters. As you can see, they were all over my body and I had to pick them out. It wasn't easy—and that was a good thing. The pain, on the other hand, was not a good thing. Since I went face-first through the door, the sharpest, longest, curliest splinters had lodged them-selves in my nose, lips, eyeballs and cheeks and each time I re-moved a splinter it was like being struck by lightning, a big bolt of spiderwhite lightning. But I kept on going. "Every splinter that comes out of you," I told myself, "is a piece of you that the splinter took from you. Now you get that piece back." Finally I'd gotten my whole body back. The body was blood-beaded from head to toe. But at least it was mine.

I cleaned myself up as best I could. I have a spry, far-reaching tongue that, when I want it to, functions not unlike a cat's tongue, as far as its ability to lick a body clean goes. I wasn't able to lick my body clean but I was able to lick it to a point that made my body look halfway presentable. That was enough for me.

DO NOT OPEN ME UP BY THROWING YOUR-SELF THROUGH ME, said the door. The sign said this, I mean, in reference to the door. Or was it in reference to itself? That is, did the word ME in the sign's message refer to the sign or the door? Perhaps it referred the word ME. Perhaps I was not supposed to open the word ME up by throwing myself through it. Then again, perhaps when the sign said ME it was referring to all of these things, the ME, the sign, the door, everything. Chances are, though, it was referring to the door and the door alone. After all, how am I supposed to throw myself through a sign no bigger than my head, let alone a tiny little word?

So why didn't the sign say: DO NOT OPEN *THE DOOR* UP BY THROWING YOURSELF THROUGH *THE DOOR*?

Well, I wasn't going to throw myself through the door this time. Not because the sign (allegedly) told me not to, nor because I would get splinters all over me again (I didn't like the pain the splinters caused but I could take it, I could take it all day and night). I just didn't want to throw myself through the door. To not throw myself through the door was my desire. My desire, founded on absolute unfoundedness. That's right. I had no reason for not throwing myself through the door and this was my reason for not throwing myself through the door. That is to say, my reason for not throwing myself through the door was that I had no reason, no reason at all, to do it. So I didn't do it. (For the record, not doing it was not an easy thing to do, it was hard, very hard, in that my will to power was not simply reacting to some other will to power that had put itself upon it. Instead, it was reacting to some other will to power that had *not* put itself upon it. Reacting to nothing, in other words, and to react to nothing is technically impossible. Thus the lack of ease in accomplishing a reaction.)

"Fucker," spat the welcome mat. It had been spitting that over and over for a minute or two, so despite the pain it caused me, which was really child's play pain now that the splinters were out of me, I stomped all over the mat with my heel until I struck and crushed its speech sensor. Then I grabbed the door by the knob, turned the knob, pushed the door open, walked through and closed it behind me.

Things are unique and meaningful only by dint of their difference to other things and when I gave my new surroundings a once over I took note of the following:

1. There's a lot of activity in this room I've walked into.
2. This must be like a cocktail party or something.
3. The wallpaper on the walls is disturbingly attractive.
4. My face is sniff-staring at a large number of hors d'oeuvres.

Not only were the hors d'oeuvres large in number, they were large in variety. There were hors d'oeuvres as upscale as potato-caviar rafts and as white trashy as Vienna sausages. There were deviled eggs, salmon and avocado pinwheel canapes, pepper brushettas, chicken wings, coronets of salami with cream cheese, sticks of celery with peanut butter, fish sticks, cheese sticks, Indonesian chicken and pineapple skewers, Tuscan prawns, French bread bowls of humus, several assortments of pate and escargots, donut holes, sausage bites, labne balls, scallop ceviches, apricot chicken puffs, black bean barbecued beef cubes, crab rolls, pigs-in-a-blanket, focaccia triangles, filo pastries, bacon-wrapped artichoke hearts, chocolate-covered cherry tomatoes, ham and cheese turnovers, fried raviolis, Chinese potstickers, shrimp stuffed pablano chilies, cheese 'n' crackers . . .

After a while I stopped taking note of the different kinds of hors d'oeuvres. This wasn't because I got sick and tired of it. It was because I suddenly took note of these two things:

1.   The hors d'oeuvres are human-sized.
2.   The human-sized hors d'oeuvres are all using martinis as a means of washing down the hors d'oeuvre-sized humans they are snacking on.

The room, perhaps as large as a basketball court, was buzzing with chatter of all timbres. There was a big martini bar at the far end of it—the bartender was a mesomorph (middle-sized human) like me—and in the middle of the room were four long tables set in a long rectangle. The tables were peppered with crystal bowls full of hors d'oeuvre-sized humans that were rapidly being consumed by the human-sized hors d'oeuvres, each of which would pick the squirming, squeaking humans up by the feet, tilt back their "heads" and drop the humans into their "mouths". The expressions on the human's faces, just before they disappeared from view, looked something like this:

Had I been anything less than a mesomorph, an endomorph (short fat person) for instance, I might have been afraid for my life. But I was quite confident that, if I was accosted, I could counteraccost and defeat the guilty party, since most of the hors d'oeuvres were shorter and much more feeble-looking than me. In fact, there was nothing feeble-looking about me at all. I am a muscular kind of person with thick, pulsing veins sticking out of certain parts of my body, not to mention how tough my newly marred face looked after being thrown through three inches of solid door . . .

I removed a cigarette I had been hiding in my armpit and lit it with a self-lighting match I had been hiding in my other armpit. I took a deep, slow drag as I moved towards the nearest table and the nearest bowl of humans. There were over 100 hors d'oeuvres at this ostensible cocktail party and none of them said anything to me until I reached the table and reached out to pick up a human. Then a Brie en croute grabbed me by the shoulder and said, "These humans are not yours to eat. They're ours to eat. Go eat your own humans."

"Yeah," added a strong-smelling cheese ball, grabbing me by the other shoulder.

Immediately I shook my shoulders free and took a step a back. I finished my cigarette in one great puff and flicked it away. Coolly placing my fists on my hips, I raised my chin a little and, exhaling two corkscrewing streams of smoke from my nostrils, said, "Your presumption, as I see it, is, in its hastiness, the epitome of all that is the antithesis of a shrewd mind. Fools! When I reached out for that bowl of humans, how did you know that my intent was to eat one or more than one of those humans, as you and all of your peers have been doing? Perhaps I just wanted to talk to one or more than one of them. Perhaps I wanted to squeeze one or more than one of them to death between my index finger and thumb. Perhaps I wanted to pick up one or more than one of them, hide one or more than one of them in my armpit, save one or more than one of them for a rainy day. Are you beginning to understand? The possibilities as to what I could and what I could not have done when I reached out for that bowl of humans—are infinite. And yet you presume that I will do just as you do! You should know that I hold you two hors d'oeuvres in the greatest contempt. You should know that, if prompted to, I can and will eat the both of you, despite your size. Your size, as a matter of fact, means nothing to me. It makes me want to eat you all the more! So then. I ask you to cease and desist, or die. Allow me to go about my business, or suffer at the greedy, sadistic hands of my teeth. I'm not joking. And I'm not making conversation for the sake of making conversation, or for any other reason either. Unless you want to be destroyed, you will leave me alone. Otherwise I'm going to wipe you out of existence. Ironically, your existence as a human-sized hors d'oeuvre is a screaming act of nihilism and so in essence by existing you cease to exist. Nevertheless, it is my belief that . . ."

Here the Brie en croute, who had been smirking throughout the entirety of my invective, began giggling aloud, and the cheese ball was quick to follow . . . as were the rest of the cocktailers, all of them. And in under a minute, every last hors d'oeuvre there was giggling at the top of their "lungs", staring and pointing at me and giggling. Then, as if that wasn't enough, the humans began giggling, and they giggled with such intensity that the crystal bowls began to vibrate like lawn mowers, and soon all of the bowls were vibrating like lawn mowers, as every single human, along with every single hors d'oeuvre, giggled hysterically at me. The only thing not giggling hysterically at me was the bartender. Silent and furrow-browed, he took the opportunity to wash and dry the little hillock of dirty martini glasses that had built up behind him.

I stood my ground the whole time. As the giggling spread across the room, I continued to stand there with my fists on my hips and my chin tilted up a little. On my face was an absolutely unaffected expression—

—that I maintained without the slightest twitch. I was a building. I was the third little pig's brick shithouse. A tornado could have blown into the cocktail party spitting livestock and machinery and farmers all over the place and I wouldn't have budged. This was the best these crummy morons could do, machine gun me with giggles? Atrocious. No: embarrassing. Embarrassing for every last giggling thing there. And for me, too. I was so embarrassed for the hor d'oeuvres and their hor d'oeuvres that I was embarrassed for myself; the knowledge that they were reacting in this way was more than enough to make my cheeks blush. Not that my cheeks blushed—I'm much stronger than that. But if I was weaker, those cheeks of mine would have been blushing all right. Giggle at me! Why not growl at me? Why not snap your teeth at me? Why not swear at me, make nasty cracks about me, spit on my shoe and backhand me, throw me on the floor and rip me to bits and pieces? It was disturbing, yes. Profoundly disturbing. I could have just exploded. But I didn't explode. I stood my ground.

And I would have kept on standing my ground until I fell over dead. Luckily, though, everybody got tired after a while. So tired, they ignored me. Apparently they had put such a great deal of emotional energy into giggling at me, they had no emotional energy left with which to acknowledge my existence. I was completely ignored. I was able to reach out for a bowl of humans untouched by hands and words, and even when I picked up and ate a human, nobody did anything. Not even the human. The human, a woman who I picked up and dropped in my palm, lay there limp, catatonic, like a raindrop of flesh; and when I popped her in my mouth and began chewing on her all she did was say "Ow" and "Shit" a few times, and in a passive tone of voice. Saddened, I swallowed her and walked over to the martini bar to get drunk, weaving through raspberry tarts, cucumber finger sandwiches, yogurt-stuffed pea pods, spam slices . . .

The bartender was wearing a plain-looking outfit and was very plain-looking himself: so plain-looking that, in his appalling plainness, he was eccentric-looking, but not so eccentric-looking that his features were worth more than three double-takes. He was still washing and drying martini glasses as I sat on a stool in front of the bar counter and pulled another cigarette and match out of my armpits. "Hello," I said and lit up.

"Never say hello," said the bartender, not looking at me. "Say hello to a stranger, no matter who they are, even if they're a bartender, *especially* if they're a bartender, and you've blown it. You've given yourself away."

"How have I given myself away?"

"Isn't it obvious? Of course it isn't. Not to you anyway. After all, you're the one that said hello! But I don't hold it against you. I don't hold anything against anybody. I'm a bartender."

"I know what you are. Give me a drink. Scotch or whisky, you pick. Doesn't matter what brand. Long as it's tall and neat."

The bartender put down the martini glass he was drying and looked up at me. At first he kind of frowned. I wondered if the frown was the result of me not being a human-sized hors d'oeuvre or of me looking like a human that had recently thrown himself through a door, but I didn't ask for clarification, and at any rate his brow quickly straightened out. "All we have are martinis," he said.

"All you have are martinis? Come on. There has to be something else back there. Doesn't there?"

The bartender looked at me.

"Fine, fine," I sighed, hitting my cigarette, "give me a dry vodka martini straight up with one olive. Kettle-One vodka, if you have it."

"All we have are sweet Beefeater gin martinis. Two olives a piece."

"All you have are *gin* martinis?"

"Sweet Beefeater gin martinis. With two olives a piece."

"That stinks."

"I'm sorry you feel that way."

"I don't believe you. I don't believe one bit of you is sorry for me."

"I'm sorry you don't believe I'm sorry for you."

"Are you? Now you're just trying to get a rise out of me. Or you're genuinely trying to console me. Whatever the case, you're making a total fool out of yourself."

"Excuse me." The bartender walked to the other end of the bar to serve a fish stick. Finishing my cigarette, I thought:

1.   This bartender is giving me a hard time.
2.   I like this bartender.
3.   I wish this bartender would quit bartending so that he could follow me around and give me a hard time for the rest of my life.

When the bartender returned to me I told him I'd have that Beefeater martini with two olives. This made him smirk. He smirked at me for fifteen seconds—a long, long time to be smirking at somebody without saying or doing anything else but smirking, in my book. I was about to tell him a little something about my book when he stopped smirking, reached into his crotch and pulled out a rocks glass of brown liquid, filled to the rim. He placed it in front of me. "Isle of Skye, that," he nodded, and started smirking again. "From my personal stash."

Before I could express my outrage—or was it gratitude I felt?—the bartender, winking at me, turned to a thirsty group of hors d'oeuvres. They ordered a large round and kept him busy for a good five minutes, during which I sipped my scotch and stared at a constellation of splinter holes on my forearm.

BED HEAD

I could hear the succubus laughing in my dream. As always, I was walking up the spinal staircase. Usually the staircase is empty or next to empty but now it was full of Harrison Ford androids. Most of them were naked, save the miniaturized Indiana Jones' whips they had threaded through the holes in their noses, ears and nipples, but a few of them were fully clothed. When I approached one of the fully clothed Harrison Fords to ask it for an autograph, its mouth creaked open like an old window and began to laugh at me in dark, icy surges. I studied the mouth for a long time, trying to see what was inside of it, before I realized that I was awake, and that the Harrison Ford was the succubus.

Growling a little, I pushed her off of me and turned over onto my side. She continued to laugh. I rolled and fell out of bed. Landed on my funny bone.

"What the hell are you laughing at?" I laughed, nursing my elbow.

"Nothing!" cackled the succubus and doubled over on the bed. Her face began to turn purple. So did mine, but for a different reason. I wanted to kill her, to rip her snake tongue out of her mouth and strangle her with it. Instead I crawled into the bathroom and took three capsules of Reality-*Plus!*

Nine seconds later I realized that the succubus didn't exist, and that if she did exist, she didn't matter. Either way she didn't exist. After I emptied myself into the toilet, I looked at my reflection in the bathroom mirror as if to confirm the realization with myself face to face.

. . . I knew there was something wrong right away, something physiognomic, but I couldn't put my finger on it. I scratched my head . . . and put my finger on it. Same as it put its finger on me.

My hair. My fingers, I mean. I mean, my hair was fingers. My skull was covered in a thick mat of long chubby fingers that, once I began to eye them, began to wiggle themselves at me. I couldn't tell if they were friendly wiggles or the kind of wiggles that say "Shame on you" or "No you don't!" There were just too many of them, too close together, all wiggling at the same time and bumping into each other. Whatever their message was they were making a mess of it. I wanted to tell them to calm down and gesticulate more clearly at me, but there were no ears on them. Whatever I said to them would not register with anyone or anything but me, so I had no reason to say anything at all. I was at the mercy of the fingers' semantic hurlyburly.

I shook a finger at my fingers and said, "Goddamn you fingers!"

"I see some thumbs up there, too," sniggered the succubus, poking her scaly head into the bathroom. "I see three, maybe four thumbs up there!" She didn't exist so I couldn't hear her, but I took some more Reality-*Plus!* anyway, because if I was consciously not hearing the succubus, then the succubus did exist, and I was hearing her loud and clear. Also I wanted to see if the Reality-*Plus!* would take care of the fingers.

It did. It took care of everything eventually. Only, by the time everything was taken care of, I had overdosed on the stuff, finished off the entire bottle, and was walking up the spinal staircase again.

This time the staircase was empty . . . except for Harrison Ford. The real one. He was lounging on a step made of glued-together femurs and tibias, sipping a Cuba Libra from a martini glass. He had gained so much weight and had become so grey, wrinkled and liver-spotted, at first I thought he was Marlon Brando. That the autograph he handed me when I walked up to him read "Brad Pitt" was even more discombobulating. But then I managed to talk him into letting me open the little control panel on his forehead. Cupping the back of his neck, I peeked inside . . . and there was no denying his true identity.

BRAIN

My brain is constantly sneaking out of me, usually right after I fall asleep at night, so that by the time I wake up in the morning it's got a big head start. Not that it matters. While I search and search for my brain, for days sometimes, in every pub, strip club and alleyway I come across, I can never find it since I'm literally air-headed and unable to unzip my fly and urinate let alone track, trap and return my brain to its rightful place. It always returns on its own anyway. It stumbles across my body in a dumpster or face down in the gutter and then worms its way back into one of my facial orifices, always drunk, always lipstick-stained, always reeking of stale smoke. If I was smart I'd fill in my ears, nostrils and mouth with cement so that my brain couldn't escape in the first place. But when my brain is gone I don't know any better. And when it's here, it's roadkill—and I don't know any better.

AT THE FUNERAL

It's been a week already and the funeral isn't over yet. For seven days and nights we've been roaming the hallways of Frinkel's Death Emporium whispering in each other's ears, massaging each other's elbows, politely trampling each other as we ransack the hors d'oeuvre table, which is replenished with a fresh round of fruit punch and cold Swedish meatballs at noon and sundown every day. The Emporium's staff consists of two short, round men in bird costumes. When they're not setting out provisions and cleaning up after us, they wobble around on their big yellow feet and make bird noises. Out of respect for our loss, they're careful not to bug us and interfere with our grief by pointing these noises at our faces.

Seven days and nights of walking around a funeral home is enough to make anybody tired, and yet nobody seems to be tired but me. I start asking people why they don't sit down for a while, maybe take a nap, but everybody just smacks their lips and waves me away.

Annoyed, I decide to look for a bed and take a nap myself. I find one in a secret room. The bed is king-sized and made out of Queen Anne's lace. On the far side of it, my sister Klarissa is sitting there playing with a doll.

In the middle of it, The Deceased is laying there dead.

The upper half of The Deceased's body is hanging out of a black, halfway unzipped body bag. He isn't wearing any clothes and His skin is absolutely colorless. His eyes look like they're on the verge of popping out of His head.

I sit down next to Him and frown at Klarissa. "Did you unzip this body bag?" I ask. She shakes her head. I say,

"You're telling me you didn't unzip this body bag? Is that what you're telling me?" She nods her head. I cock mine. Then I say, "Well, I guess the thing unzipped itself. I guess that's what happened, isn't it?" This time my sister doesn't respond to me. She whispers something into her doll's ear and giggles.

Ignoring her, I use my feet to try and stuff The Deceased back into the body bag, but it doesn't work, and when I'm about to lay my hands on Him, my mother walks into the secret room, scolds my sister and I for being there, then sits down on the bed and places The Deceased's head in her lap. She strokes His curly brown hair. A few seconds later . . . He coughs.

"Holy moly," I say.

My mother closes her eyes. "No, no. That's just a reflex."

"Reflex? He's been dead over a week."

Now my mother rolls her eyes. I make a bitter face. My mother begins to massage The Deceased's neck. The Deceased coughs again. Then, purring a little, He mumbles, "That feels good."

Before I can say anything my mother looks at me and says, "Reflexes. It's all reflexes." I stare at her. My mother shrugs. "Listen, I have to go. Aunt Gretchen's been feeding meatballs to the spiders and I have to try and convince her to feed them to herself instead. You two can stay here for now, but don't let me catch you in here later, okay? Be good." She removes The Deceased's head from her lap, gets off the bed and leaves.

The Deceased flexes His jaw. He coughs again, and again, and again. He keeps on coughing until a rotten apple flies out of His mouth and across the room. It nails an antique lamp, shatters it. Klarissa and I leap off the bed as The Deceased starts gesticulating like an angry worm. "Get me outta this damn thing," He says.

"I don't think that's such a good idea," I reply. Klarissa adds, "We might get in trouble." Then, under her breath: "Is this a reflex, too?"

I purse my lips.

The Deceased gives us a dirty look. "Fine. I'll get out myself. And I'll never forgive you two for being so crummy to me."

Klarissa and I glance at each other. After a brief struggle, The Deceased manages to unzip the body bag the rest of the way. He climbs out of it. He stretches His wiry, naked limbs, rearranges His genitals and strides out of the secret room without a word. Klarissa and I watch Him go.

Then we leap back onto the bed and take naps on either side of the open body bag.

Out in the hallways The Deceased approaches the attendants of the funeral, one at a time. He taps them on the shoulders and asks them if they can spare some clothes and if it's not too much trouble a meatball and a cup of fruit punch, too. "I'm very cold and undernourished," He says, eyes fixed on his toes. But everybody just frowns at Him and pretends they don't understand Him, except for my Aunt Gretchen, who, in response to His plea, spits a mouthful of tobacco juice on Him and then shoots up into the ceiling on a thread of spidersilk attached to the back of her neck. The Deceased breaks down and cries. When He gets tired of crying, He starts swearing at everybody. He keeps on swearing until my grandfather threatens to have Him hanged. "We'll string you up right here and won't even think twice about it!" my grandfather twangs. The Deceased snarls at him. My grandfather snarls back, then signals the Emporium's two bird men and they all chase The Deceased back to the secret room and tell Him not to come out again unless He wants to die.

"I'm already dead," says The Deceased as my grandfather slams the door on His face.

Klarissa and I are fast asleep and don't wake up. The Deceased shuffles over to the bed. He stares at us and thinks about what He should do. Should He kill us? Should He maim us? Or should He just leave us alone? Since He dislikes us so much, the most sensible thing to do would be to kill us. But He can't make up His mind. He tries to wake us and ask us to make up His mind for Him. No luck—we're sleeping like dead things. No matter how hard He pokes our shoulders and screams in our ear holes, we won't open our eyes.

The Deceased sighs. Then, having nothing else to do, He crawls onto the bed and back into the body bag, and zips Himself up as best He can.

THE MAN IN THE THICK BLACK SPECTACLES

Before opening the door and entering the conference room, the man in the thick black spectacles removed the wad of chewing gum from his mouth and, after glancing in every imaginable direction, stuck it into an unassuming, seemingly clean crack in the wall. He would retrieve the gum from the crack later, after the meeting, which would take no more and no less than five minutes. He knew this for three reasons:

1. This morning the man in the cubicle next door had told him so.
2. There was a neon billboard hanging from the ceiling of the office that read:

> MEETING TODAY
> 5 MINUTES LONG
> NO MORE, NO LESS

3. Of the countless meetings he had attended before, he could not remember one of them being more or less than five minutes.

So there was no reason why this meeting should be any different, and no reason why the man in the thick black spectacles should be worried.

And yet he was worried. Five minutes was five minutes, after all.

He placed a fingernail between his teeth and began to

chew on it. What if, say, a fly landed on the gum while he was away? He would have no way of knowing what the fly had done to the gum in his absence. For all he knew, the fly would crap on it, meaning that the man in the thick black spectacles, in the not-too-distant future, might very well be chewing on fly dung. This was not a pretty thought so he tried not to think it, or to think thoughts like it. He couldn't allow himself to. To allow himself to think that way would be distracting, and this meeting, while short, was, like all of the other meetings, an important one. It required that he be sharp as a tack.

Removing the fingernail from his teeth, he opened the door . . . and hesitated, unable to help himself, despite himself.

Five minutes, he thought. Sometimes one minute seems like an eternity, especially when you're thinking about that minute. It's one thing to handle one minute, or rather, one eternity. But can I handle *five* of them?

Eyeing the gum, he clicked his tongue and stroked his brow. He sighed. Closing the door, he looked back over his right shoulder, his left shoulder, his right shoulder. Then he looked between his legs, underneath his shoes . . .

Hardly satisfied, but more anxious now about hesitating and being late for the meeting than abandoning the gum, the man in the thick black spectacles walked in at last, closing the door behind him slowly, guardedly, without a sound, pulling his beaklike nose inside just as the door clicked shut.

Immediately the man in the silver handlebar mustache unfolded his appendages and snuck out from behind the water cooler. Giggling, he crept over to the crack in the wall. He stretched out his long neck, rolled out his tongue and began to lap at the gum as a thirsty dog might lap at a bowl of water.

At the same time the man in the neon zoot suit wormed his way up from out of the soil in the pot that contained the office's largest rubber plant, using the branches of the plant for leverage, but still, this worming took a while and by the time he was free of the soil and had dusted himself off, the man in the silver handlebar mustache was fully engaged, his tongue lapping at high speed. The man in the neon zoot suit would have to wait his turn. Being the impatient sort, he couldn't stop himself from cursing, albeit he did so in an undertone. But after a while the man in the flamingo pink top hat fell through a ceiling tile with a crash and at least the man in the neon zoot suit had some company now. He stopped cursing . . . until the man in the flamingo pink top hat started cursing, first because he had fallen, second because of the man in the silver handlebar mustache, who was taking too long, far too long, who was hogging the wad of chewing gum all too himself!

Not a moment passed before the man in the neon zoot suit joined his estranged colleague in blasphemous harmony. "Why not give us a go, you filthy bastard?" they bitched. The man in the silver handlebar mustache promptly sucked his tongue back into his mouth, stood upright and about-faced. To his aggressors he replied, "If one wants something, all one has to do is ask. That's all one has to do."

The sarcasm in the man in the silver handlebar mustache's tone of voice was flagrant enough but neither the man in the neon zoot suit nor the man in the flamingo pink top hat had ever cared enough about sarcasm to be able to detect it, even if it slapped them across both cheeks. Muttering hasty thankyous under their breath, they attacked the crack in the wall at the same time, smacked into each other and collapsed to the floor. They got to their feet and blinked. Following a brief, woozy exchange, they played rock-paper-scissors to see who between them got to lick the gum first.

The man in the flamingo pink top hat won.

"Balls!" exclaimed the loser; he ripped the peacock's feather out of his tando hat and stomped on it as the victor, with the tip of a sharp tongue, began stabbing at the gum, again and again, growing more excitable and outrageous with each snake-like stab. The man in the silver handlebar mustache, now leaning up against the wall with arms crossed, sniggered, then began moving his tongue around the insides of his mouth so that his cheeks kept poking out. He smacked his lips, too, each time glaring derisively at the man in the neon zoot suit out of the corners of his eyes.

Finally the man in the neon zoot suit had had enough. Being twice as tall and twice as strong as the man in the flamingo pink top hat and the man in the silver handlebar mustache combined, but always hesitant to resort to his brawn until the last straw had been drawn, which it had, which it most definitely had—he backhanded the man in the flamingo pink top hat away from the wall and sent him sliding down the hallway on his spine, his arms and legs and sharp tongue waving in the air like the extremities of an overturned beetle. Then he pointed an angry warning finger at the man in the silver handlebar mustache, but all that man was doing was whistling a quiet tune and feigning a reverie. This irked the man in the neon zoot suit but not enough to lead his one-track mind astray; he just pressed a finger to one nostril and out the other nostril blasted out an ornery little snot ball and then he opened up his shark mouth and turned and made for the gum that the man in the thick black spectacles had stuck right there in the crack in the wall . . . but too late, too late. The door to the conference room was being opened up, slowly, guardedly, without a sound, and in a flash the man in the silver handlebar mustache had folded himself up behind the water cooler again, and the man in the flamingo pink top hat had both rallied from the backhand and leapt back up into the ceiling, replacing the tile he had fallen through with a fresh one. So the man in the neon zoot suit was all alone. And when the man in the thick black spectacles emerged, it was he and no other that would be to blame, despite his innocence. For while the man in the neon zoot suit had certainly wanted to lick the gum, and would have licked it if he could have—and the gum had clearly been licked, a forensics expert wasn't needed to figure that out—the truth of the matter was: he had not licked anything.

At this point the man in the neon zoot suit asked himself three simple questions. He would have asked himself more, but time wouldn't permit it.

1. What is to become of me once I get caught?
2. Will the man in the thick black spectacles attack me or give me the opportunity to explain myself?
3. Given the opportunity, how will I explain myself?

The man in the neon zoot suit was about to ask himself a fourth question when something overcame him, something that, when he reflected on it later during a water cooler conversation with the man in the silver handlebar mustache and the man in the flamingo pink top hat, he described as an "impulsive burst of energy" that allowed him to spring up and across the hallway, dive back down into the soil of the rubber plant and cover himself over just enough so that nobody would take note of his stealth. "It was a brilliant move," he bragged.

"And yet quite unnecessary," smiled the man in the silver handlebar mustache.

The man in the flamingo pink top hat added, "Yes. Quite unnecessary."

When the man in the neon zoot suit said, "I don't get it," the man in the flamingo pink top hat, who had seen everything through a mouse hole in the ceiling, told him. "As it so happened," he said, "the man in the thick black spectacles, after slipping out the door that led into the conference room, was apparently so preoccupied he forgot all about his gum. He stood there in the hallway a moment, nervously fingering an ear lobe and flexing his jowls. Then he spent some time making these sickly croaking noises. I suspected he was either about to faint or have a heart attack and die, but just as this suspicion crept into my mind he bleated like a sheep that's been sat upon by a fat man. Finally he scurried off, down the hallway, talking to himself in a worried voice. And that's that."

"That's that," repeated the man in the neon zoot suit in a dull whisper, then turned with a quick jerk, like a man that wants to be alone with his dread.

DETAILS OF A CONFERENCE ROOM

The conference room is shaped like a clown face. In the middle of it is a table, also the shape of a clown face. The light fixtures on the ceiling are not shaped like clown faces, they are clown faces, clown faces that gaze down on the table with flashing florescent eyes and grins.

There are chairs surrounding the conference room's table. The chairs are bound in human skin and the humans sitting in them—it is their own skin that binds them, all of the glistening, blood-colored humans sit in their own skin.

And as the humans sit there, they stare at Mr. Void.

Mr. Void is sitting in the middle of the table in a tight ball. Sometimes he will sit there for a minute, sometimes for a year; whatever the duration, he won't move a muscle, won't even take a breath. Then, suddenly, without warning, Mr. Void will roll to this or that end of the table and a finger-pointing hand will emerge from the ball and fall on one of the humans surrounding him, accusing them.

On the ledge outside the conference room's one window is a window-sized photograph of the conference room and all of its goings-on. Outside the conference room's one door, on the other hand, is a door-sized circus mirror.

THE BEEF TIPS

The arena is perfectly round and the plain, unpainted stucco wall that surrounds it is no taller than a man. Beyond the wall is where the audience sits. Within the wall, in the middle of the arena, is where a little pile of beef tips sits. They are old and cold, these beef tips, but not one of them is uncooked or rotten. It is all right to eat them.

"Don't eat those," commands The Nihilist. He's wearing a heavily starched, hunter green The Nihilist uniform and has a flashy inverted Hitler mustache (smooth in the middle with wild handlebars on the sides). "I say, don't you eat those beef tips. Those beef tips do not exist and if you eat them they will eat you. That is to say, if you eat them you will cease to exist. And you will not only cease to exist now, you will have never existed in the first place, just like those beef tips do not exist now or in the past—or, for that matter, in the future. In any event, what I'm saying is, don't eat those goddamned things. I forbid it. Okay?" The Nihilist raises an eyebrow. It is only he and I (and the little pile of beef tips of course) in the arena and when I fail to respond to him he clacks his heels together, thrusts his hand up into the air and salutes me; thinking this gesture, in its show of respect, will force me into submission. But I am not the kind to submit. Even though the vast audience surrounding the arena, every single one of them a The Nihilist impressionist wearing a The Nihilist uniform and inverted Hitler mustache, follows his lead and salutes me—I am not the kind to submit. On the contrary, I am the kind to defy, to aggress, to antagonize. To eat little piles of beef tips when The Nihilist tells me not to! And if those beef tips have the power to wipe me out of existence, fine: I will still exist insofar as my existence will be characterized by my non-existence. Either way, I will exist.

As my naked body dances across the clay floor of the arena toward the beef tips, The Nihilist begins to pace back and forth, moving no more than two steps in one direction before pivoting on his heel and moving in the opposite direction, and as he does this he gesticulates and gripes and shakes his head and blinks his eyes in disbelief. The members of the audience, in turn, begin applying heavy doses of lard to the handlebars of their mustaches and twisting and molding them into all kinds of odd origami-looking shapes, trying as best they can not to think about what I am about to do. To think about what I am about to do, they are telling themselves, is unthinkable. Unthinkable! And if the unthinkable is thought . . . No! I will not think it! I will twist and mold my mustache—nothing more!

The beef tips are soon within my grasp but I hesitate, captivated by one of the The Nihilist impressionist's mustaches. He's perched on top of the wall of the arena and has shaped his mustache into the image of the singer/actress Madonna. Actually, there are two Madonnas emerging from either side of his overlip by their pony tails, two nude, life-sized, lard-colored Madonnas that stretch down and out from these pony tails and sit beside him on the left and right with their legs spread not too wide, but wide enough. The amount of lard that went into the construction of these fine monstrosities must be considerable, not to mention that the bush of his mustache must be of Nietzschean proportions, and I want to go over to the impressionist and commend him on his craftsmanship. But that's just what he wants me to do, the bastard. Anything to draw me away from the allegedly non-existent beef tips. And it is illegal to approach an impressionist anyway, even if the intent of your approach is good-willed. The penalty for doing such a thing is the surgical removal of the guilty party's arms, and if the guilty party's arms have, like mine, already been surgically removed, then it's the legs that are to go. So not only is this impressionist trying to keep me from the beef tips, he's trying to hack my legs out from under me! Shifting all of my body weight onto my left heel and arching my spine just so, I lift up my right leg and point my big toe at him, and stare hard and wide-eyed at him, to let him know that I *know* what he's trying to do to me with those open-legged Madonnas, the breasts of which are now being caressed by his delirious fingers. Then I pivot on my left heel and point at The Nihilist, who is still storming back and forth in a crazed, spasmodic huff. But when I point at him he freezes. Everybody freezes.

"This is your last warning," The Nihilist says, his expression the quintessence of terror. "I'm telling you, this is it. If you don't listen to me . . . but you'll listen to me. Won't you? You have to listen to me. Don't you? Don't you know who I am? I am The Nihilist!" He stands there rigid now, glowering at me. He's still terrified but it's obvious that calling himself The Nihilist out loud alleviated that terror a bit. When he sees that my leg and pointing toe and wide hard eyes remain poised, however, the terror returns en masse and he begins making quiet, pleading, melodramatic gestures with his hands and face, like an actor in a silent film. The audience follows suit. Within seconds virtually every The Nihilist impressionist is moving about as if they might be in a silent film, too, making constipated faces, bearing mouthfuls of gnashing teeth, bugging out their eyeballs, clutching and slashing at the air . . . Intrigued, I watch them go on like this for a while. Then the intrigue wears off and I lower my leg. The leg has fallen asleep so I have to wait a moment for the prickly feeling to go away before I can turn and fall on and devour the little pile of beef tips. They taste good, even though they are old and cold, and I finish them in just a few bites and swallows. It's difficult to eat things when you don't have any arms, especially if those things are lying on the ground in a pile. I manage, though.

Licking my lips, I stand back up, belch an echoing belch, and face The Nihilist . . . But it isn't The Nihilist. It's The Pantheist. He's wearing a heavily starched, navy blue The Pantheist uniform and has a dark, pencil thin mustache. Appropriately, the audience is full of The Pantheist impressionists, each wearing the same uniform and mustache. My first instinct is to ask The Pantheist what happened to The Nihilist. But once I notice the little pile of old, cold (but not uncooked or rotten) chicken strips sitting in the very middle of the arena, I suppress my instinct and wait, patiently, for The Pantheist to give me his directive.

THE STRANGER IN THE MANHOLE

We were picking up speed at a dangerous rate. All I could do was shove my hands beneath my ass and squeeze, digging in with my fingernails, replacing the fear with pain.

"Get out of here," hissed Leete for the third time. "I wanna do this by myself. How many times I hafta tell you? Besides, you're always hanging around. I'm tired of it—and *you*. Now get out!"

Leete was an old friend and I was used to this sort of abuse. Usually I would have abused him right back, but I was in no condition to argue right now. So before it was too late, before we accelerated to the point of no return (or, in this case, the point of no departure), I did what I was told. Removing my hands from my ass I gave the door handle a yank and with a mad shriek hurled my body out of the car. I rolled, the world spinning and whistling. When I came to a stop on the cool concrete floor of the warehouse, I blundered to my feet and waited for the dizziness to pass, then climbed a nearby cardboard building—mirrored windows had been painted all over its towering but flimsy bulk so my reflection never left me alone during my climb—and on the building's rooftop arranged myself in an Indian-style sitting position.

Still a little anxious, but as comfortable as I was going to get, I took a survey the warehouse. It was immense. As spacious as a small city, although there was really nobody around but us and a few strangers scattered here and there. And the strangers were bastards. All they did, if they weren't hiding somewhere, was push buildings and houses and things all over the place and upset the topography of the warehouse, so that people like me were always getting lost; and even when they were busying themselves in this way they could rarely be seen, since most of them took great care in placing the objects that they were moving between themselves and their watchers. Strangely, though, I could see one of the strangers now. It was the first stranger I had seen in a long time. He was poking his head up from out of a distant manhole and making sour faces at me, but at the same time giggling wildly, as if the lime he might be sucking on was the funniest lime he had ever put in his mouth. Was this a kind gesture? Was it an attempt on the stranger's part to befriend me? I waved. He didn't acknowledge me; he continued with his faces and his hilarity. I stood up, threw down my pants, turned around and mooned him, and stared eagerly at him through my legs, searching for a reaction. Nothing. I pulled my pants up and sat back down again, this time hugging my knees to my chest. I frowned at the stranger, shook my head at him in disappointment. I was about to yell something at him when I heard the crash.

Jarred, I let go of my knees, rocked back and sprung to my feet—the building beneath me teetered and I had to wait for it to settle—then peered down over the edge of the rooftop at the two smashed-up cars. One was the cherry-red Ferrari I had bailed out of, the other was the metallic grey Porsche the Ferrari had been playing chicken with.

It took a little while for the passengers to emerge from the wreck, but eventually they crawled and snaked and grunted their way out of the twisted, smoking mess of metal.

"You shithead!" Leete shouted up at me, spotting me right away. The proprietor of the once-was Porsche, a wiry individual with tousled silver hair and skin the color of an old bone that went by the name of Mr. Shadowpain, stood at Leete's side, nodding in grave silence.

To Leete I said, "Don't blame me. It's not my fault,

what you did. Chicken. What kind of dumbass plays chicken? Anyway you told me to get out. So I did. You can't blame me for doing what you told me to do."

Leete tugged ruminatively at an ear lobe. "I'm drunk?" he said and lifted an eyebrow.

"You're stupid," I replied.

Leete made his hands into fists and threw them down at his sides. His cheeks flared. "Get down here, you! This is crazy. Can't we talk about this like real people? Why do you hafta be so difficult?"

"I'm not being difficult," I said, "I just think you're a bunch of bullshit and I'm sick of it. You're supposed to be my friend, but you don't act like it. Not ever. What the hell's the matter with you? What kind of—"

"Every facet of life is a form of psychological warfare," interrupted Leete, who lashed out with this maxim every single time he backed himself into a corner, which was often, far too often, and I said, "Blow it out your ass." At that Leete began screaming at me. I waited patiently for him to finish. When he didn't, I removed my penis from my pants and urinated on his head. The cardboard building wasn't too tall, but it wasn't too short either, maybe 100 feet from the ground up, so by the time my stream of piss got down there, it had spread out, like buckshot, and some of it got on one of Mr. Shadowpain's shoulders. This absolutely infuriated Leete. Mr. Shadowpain was new to the warehouse and Leete and I didn't know him very well, but this didn't stop Leete from carrying on like the child he was. Stomping in place, he tore at his bright platinum hair and gnashed his brighter platinum teeth until Mr. Shadowpain quieted him by raising a slow ashen hand and motioning him over to his Porsche's trunk, the only part of that car that hadn't been demolished. Mr. Shadowpain pushed a button on his keychain, there was a high-pitched beep, and the trunk popped open.

"Get him," he said with venom, pointing up at me . . . and out of the trunk poured a demonic throng of homunculi.

I gasped. The homunculi were nude, earless, entirely hairless. A gelatinous, placenta-like substance ooze-dripped off of their luminous white bodies. They were still dazed from the accident, it seemed—each homunculus staggered and swayed as it approached the cardboard building—but at the same time I could tell they were more than capable of that which they had apparently been trained to do. Like lunatic insects they grabbed hold of the building and began scuttling up it, snarling, farting, snapping their over-developed fangs. I was afraid that the building, given its consistency, wouldn't be able to support their weight and would give way long before the homunculi were all over me. But the building didn't give way. And the homunculi kept on coming. And Leete, not surprisingly, reveled in my misfortune.

There happened to be a junk pile next to the cardboard building, tall and very thin, its peak parallel with the building's rooftop. Leete scampered up to this peak with such speed and agility that the junk pile didn't even budge, let alone fall over. All of a sudden there he was, tippy-toe on an old rotten shoe. He said, "You're in for it now, my friend," and smiled a haughty smile. I ignored him. I also ignored the snarls and farts and snaps of the approaching homunculi, and the vibrations of the building beneath me, which grew more and more treacherous by the second. But I could have cared less. I had accepted my fate, for now at least, and so I sat down and began whistling, waiting for whatever was going to happen to happen.

As I whistled, I looked out across the warehouse again, squinting to see if he was still there, way out there, the stranger in the manhole, still giggling and making those faces at me. But in the last few minutes another stranger had pushed a small house over the manhole and covered it.

THE EAGLE-HEADED MAN AT THE AIRPORT

No, Socius Protagynism doesn't like to fly. Just the thought of being strapped into a moving, airborne plane fills him with dread and produces little ocean surfs in his palms and armpits. It's the turbulence that gets to him more than anything, the sometimes minute, sometimes monstrous, always antagonizing bump and grind of a hundred ton hunk of metal colliding with this or that ill-tempered headwind. Turbulence—it's his enemy. But so is the possibility that the airplane he has paid a disgustingly extravagant amount of money to sit in will at any moment hit an air pocket and freefall a thousand feet. Or explode. Or run nose first into another airplane and explode. Or maybe there's a trap door underneath his disgustingly uncomfortable seat that will open if he reaches up to the ceiling and presses the steward button. Will he remain conscious as his body flaps to the ground at the speed of a bullet, or will he freeze to death in the arctic cold of 30,000 feet long before his body strikes the earth and shatters? He hopes he freezes to death. He hopes, after the plane explodes and sets his body on fire, the freezing cold puts both his life and the fire out, albeit if his life is put out it doesn't matter if the fire is subsequently put out or not, does it. So many possibilities. *Possibility*. That's what really fills Socius Protagynism with dread. He knows flying is the safest means of travel but the possibility that something might go grotesquely wrong is always-already there. And he's powerless against it. He's Possibility's whore. Driving a car is far more dangerous than flying in an airplane, yes, he knows this, he's not stupid, he's fairly intelligent and perspicacious actually, but the fact remains, when he's driving a car at least *he's driving the car* and his

life is more or less in his own sweat-soaked hands. In an airplane, however, his life is in the (dry? sweat-soaked? if so, how
sweat-soaked?) hands of two or three or four pilots who he knows
absolutely nothing about and who he never sees, unless they
decide to poke their heads out of the cockpit and say hi to him
as he boards and deboards the airplane, a rare occurrence in
Socius Protagynism's experience. Who are these people? And
why aren't copies of their pilot degrees and credentials and character references passed out to the passengers before takeoff?
Perhaps they're not pilots at all. No way to prove it, not without
the proper documentation. They could be anybody. They could
be a shit-faced heavy metal band, for all Socius Protagynism
knows. And his life—they control it. A bunch of total strangers are in charge of Socius Protagynism's existence, everything
he is and was and ever will be. The thought makes him bite the
insides of his cheeks until they bleed, bleed in synch with the
tears that are beginning to flow down the outsides of his cheeks,
tears of fear, tears of bitterness, tears of regret, ultimately tears of
self-pity and he wishes he was nicer to people and closer to the
Lord his God Jesus Christ and he should be doing charity work
of some kind on a regular basis (at an old folks home? a home-
less shelter? a children's hospital? a mental institution?) and suddenly, swallowing his blood and wiping his cheeks, he stands
up. Grabs his carry-on and darts into the nearest bar, a Cheers.
His plane leaves in just under an hour and in five minutes he is
served five shots of Chivas by a Ted Danson lookalike and he
pounds the shots bang bang bang bang bang then darts out of
Cheers and through a crowd and out sliding doors and ten minutes later he has chainsmoked half a pack of cigarettes . . . Ah
yes. Now it doesn't matter if the pilots are heroine-snorting
rock stars. Nor does it matter if his plane bursts into flames. He
would prefer his plane bursts into flames, in fact, because then
he would be the only one not screaming and crying and acting

like a baby. Unlike all of the other passengers, he would die like a man, blank-faced and burning, freezing, falling—passed out drunk.

But before he passed out drunk he had to get on the plane. And in any case it took a lot more than five scotches and half a pack of cigarettes to put him on his ass: Socius Protagynism was no stranger to the drink and the smoke. Fact is, he was hardly even buzzed. But he did feel a little more relaxed. Not quite relaxed enough to die like a man, he realized, but relaxed enough to not focus solely on the fact that Possibility was caving in on him. He couldn't ask for more. Things could be worse, after all. Things could always be a whole lot worse.

How much time before takeoff? Better get to the gate . . .

Very crowded, the airport. Abnormally so. Travelers buzzed and flowed, buzzed and flowed to the sound of clicking heels and tiny rolling wheels, and every few minutes unseen loudspeakers burped and a metallic voice said, "Attention please. Do not leave your luggage unattended. It is forbidden. It is against the law. If, however, you do leave your luggage unattended, report yourself to the nearest law enforcer at once. You will not get in trouble. Law enforcers will not reprimand, be cynical with or beat you. At most they will search and destroy your luggage and demand you pay a small fine. Nobody likes fines. So why not do the right thing and keep a sharp eye on your luggage?"

Socius Protagynism sat upright on the end of a long string of plastic bucket chairs, which were facing the fluid main drag of Terminal D, and listened to the loudspeakers. His hands were neatly folded in his lap and his chin was resting on the shoulder adjacent his carry-on, a small black leather satchel resembling a bowling ball bag. It was sitting in the bucket seat next to him. He was staring at it. Directly at it, with the intensity of somebody trying to discern the movement of the short hand of a clock. He would not look away. He was a staunch law abider and if he looked away he would have to turn himself in . . . unless, that is, he looked away and kept the bag in his peripheral gaze. Should he do it? He spent some time deliberating what might be gained by doing it and concluded that nothing, nothing at all might be gained, he would be much better off, in the grand scheme of things, keeping his eyes and his head where they were. To not keep his eyes and his head where they were—it wasn't in his best interests.

Socius Protagynism didn't always do what was in his best interests. Even when he was stone sober. And especially when he was about to—fly.

Slowly he removed his chin from his shoulder and rotated the chin 45 degrees. Four tries, it took him. The first three tries he got no further than 20 degrees before chickening out and quickly returning his chin and eyes to their original position, cursing himself as a fool, then as a coward. On the first three tries the prospect of his foolishness outweighed the certainty of his cowardice. The fourth try, however, saw him come to the conclusion that it was better to be a fool than a coward, and he successfully executed a 45 degree rotation of the head and eyes.

He was staring straight ahead now at a thick cascade of people in trench coats and Hawaiian t-shirts and priestly robes and turbans and handlebar mustaches and pumps and tank tops, but his attention remained on his carry-on. He couldn't conceive of his attention being elsewhere. Even if a screeching baboon fell out of the ceiling into his lap, the object of his gaze would remain constant. It must remain constant. He owed it to himself as much as to the passengers that would be joining him on his flight.

"Attention please. Do not leave your luggage unattended. It is forbidden. It is against the law. If, however . . ."

Despite his firm resolve to be attentive to the object warranting his attentiveness, it was not long, not long at all, before Socius Protagynism asked himself the following question: Should I disengage my peripheral attention from my carry-on?

Nobody would know. Nobody *had* to know. Except . . . him. He would know and that was enough. Wasn't it? If he disregarded his bag, which was sitting right next to him, right there on the seat next to his own, for, say, twenty seconds . . . really, what could happen in twenty seconds? Nobody was even sitting or standing in his general vicinity. And the probability that somebody was watching him was low, very very low. He was a plain enough looking joe, wasn't he? But even if somebody was watching him—the eagle-headed man over by the kiosk, for instance—they probably weren't watching him consistently. They were probably just setting their sights on him for a few seconds at a time, for a few seconds every three minutes or so, then directing their sights to the next plain-looking joe, and the next one, and the next one, until all of the plain-looking joes had been looked at and it was his turn again. The point is, there was a very good chance that, if Socius Protagynism closed his eyes for, well, let's say fifteen seconds, nothing would happen, not to him, not to his bag. The eagle-headed man was too far away to tell if he closed his eyes anyway: Socius Protagynism knew this because he had 20/20 vision and couldn't tell whether or not the eagle-headed man's eyes were open or closed, although his alert posture was evidence of his eyes being open. Still, he couldn't prove it. Not from his vantage point. And so there was no way the eagle-headed man, who may or may not have had 20/20 vision, even with the aid of contact lenses, could, from his vantage point, prove the same.

"Attention please. Do not leave your luggage unattended. It is for . . ."

But why is Socius Protagynism even considering closing his eyes? Why would he want to do that?

(Why did he reduce his view of his carry-on from a direct to a peripheral view in the first place?)

. . . On the ninth second of the fifteen seconds that Socius Protagynism had his eyes closed—like the first episode it took him a number of tries to accomplish the full fifteen seconds—he decided he would turn himself in. If he didn't, he wouldn't be able to live with himself, let alone fly, despite his lack of sobriety. He hadn't sensed or heard anything or anybody fooling with his bag while his eyes were closed, but his eyes had been closed, so there was no way to prove that his bag had come out of the ordeal untouched. For all he knew a quick, covert passerby had opened his bag and thrown a ticking time bomb in there and closed it, all in a matter of seconds, and if Socius Protagynism got on his plane with that bag and if that bomb was in there he would be responsible for the deaths of 200+ people. It wasn't likely. It was highly unlikely. But it was a possibility. A very disturbing, very real possibility.

Possibility.

Socius Protagynism considered unzipping his bag and checking its contents. Then he considered that it might be wired to blow by means of the zipper and, unfolding his hands from his lap, he stood and carefully picked up the bag . . . and hurried it all the way over to the eagle-headed man, with an agonized expression on his face, holding it out in front of him like a pile of excrement he was trying to keep from falling apart. As he went he artfully weaved through people in suits and ties, bell bottoms, beehive hairdos, wrinkled up ponchos, moon boots, ear muffs, cut off jeans . . .

"Hello," said Socius Protagynism, out of breath. "Hello hello. Whew. I need to tell you something. I'm going to tell you something. Just let me catch my breath a second."

As Socius Protagynism, still holding his carry-on out in front of him in the eagle-headed man's face (but not so much in his face that he slapped it away), caught his breath, the eagle-headed man blinked at him. His back was flush against the brick wall next to the kiosk, which was being attended by a chubby Puerto Rican girl who phased in and out of sleep as people approached her to make a purchase. The eagle-headed man was wearing worn-out jeans and a worn-out denim button-down shirt that was tightly tucked into his jeans, accentuating his powerful chest. His face was as sharp and birdlike as sharp, birdlike faces come and his hands hung at his sides, awkwardly, as if they wanted to be shoved into his pockets but he was denying them the privilege.

"You're eyes are open," breathed Socius Protagynism, smiling in triumph. The eagle-headed man blinked at him. Socius Protagynism wiped the smile off his face and said, "Well, yeah, I guess I better get to the point. I guess I better. I mean, you're probably wondering . . . well, you're probably wondering, is all. But hold on." As he cannily lowered his carry-on from the eagle-headed man's face and tucked it under an arm, firmly gripping the handle of the bag with the hand of his other arm, the eagle-headed man said nothing, nor did he make an effort to elude or shoo away the stranger that had accosted him and was presumably about to accost him further. He didn't flinch. All he did was stand there against the wall with his hands dangling and his eyes blinking . . . which led Socius Protagynism to believe, now more than ever, that the eagle-headed man was the man he needed to consult.

"Thanks for your patience," said Socius Protagynism, "I'll try to be as brief as possible. Let's see, how should I proceed? Hm. I don't know. I don't know quite where to begin. Uhhhh . . . (series of awkward nasal chuckles) . . . See, the thing is, I'm trying to figure out the best, most expeditious way to tell you what I need, and want, to tell you, without getting tangled up in a lot of rhetorical red tape, you know? But I guess I've already tangled up myself a little haven't I. I guess I'm tangling myself up just by talking about how I'm not going to tangle myself up, or rather about how my strategy consists of me not tangling myself up. But I'm tangled. I'm tangled as hell. And I'm becoming more and more tangled with each passing moment. I should just stop dwelling on how tangled up I am and come out and say that which I am prepared to say to you. I'm going to do that, in order to insure that this tangled existence I've created for myself, and you for that matter, ceases to be. Well, it'll never cease to be, I mean, it's out there, it happened, but that doesn't mean we can't move forward. So. Let's move forward. Can we move forward please? Sorry, I'm drunk. Kind of. Actually I'm hardly buzzed. Five shots back to back, too. How about that?"

The eagle-headed man blinked again, but he also shifted about uneasily, prompting Socius Protagynism to get to the point, but not before cursing himself inwardly for not getting to the point right off the bat.

"I left my bag unattended," said Socius Protagynism and waited for a response. There was no response. "No response?" he said, more to himself than to the eagle-headed man. He clicked his tongue. "I see. Well, I guess you need to hear a little more than what I've told you. I can understand that. You need details. How my bag came to be unattended, for instance, and how long, once unattended, it persisted in being unattended, and under what circumstances, and where exactly did this state of unattendedness take place? But you know where it took place, don't you. Of course you do. And I bet you know a lot more. I'd put money on it, if I had any. Well, I have some money but not enough to make me feel comfortable gambling. Anyway what I did was—and you know this, I know you know this, but I'm going to tell you anyway, the very nature of confession demands I open my mouth and tell you—what I did was . . . oh but you know what I did. You know! You saw what I did over there . . . right? I have 20/20 vision, you see, and I couldn't see whether or not you were seeing me. But I have a feeling about you. I have a feeling your vision is superior to 20/20 vision. Do you have optical implants in there? I wouldn't doubt it. Yes, you know exactly what's going on here, *exactly* what's going on here, so I'm going to give you this piece of carry-on luggage tucked beneath my arm. Unzip it, open it, and check its contents. I want you to. I also want you to incarcerate me, if you think it's necessary. If you don't think it's necessary, though, I'd prefer not to be incarcerated. But do whatever you have to do. Cuff me, I don't care. I left my bag unattended and guess what: *I did it on purpose.* On purpose! The opportunity to *not* attend to my bag—it was there and I took it. Took it, an reveled in it. And now I'm prepared to pay the piper. Here."

Socius Protagynism removed his carry-on from his underarm and, once again, shoved it in the eagle-headed man's face.

The eagle-headed man reacted by cocking back his head a little and doling out the proverbial series of blinks, although this series, unlike all those preceding it, was quicker and more erratic, no doubt because Socius Protagynism's move was swift and unexpected, even though he did say "Here" before executing the move. But then the eagle-headed man stopped blinking altogether. And his eyes widened into perfect circles, frightening Socius Protagynism at first, but thirty seconds later—not a word or gesture was exchanged between the two men during these thirty seconds, they remained there the whole time, the eagle-headed man against the wall, Socius Protagynism holding the bag in his face, the steady thunderhum of the busybodied airport resonating all around them—the affect of the wide, un-blinking eyes wore off and he wanted to tell him to blink, otherwise his eyes were going to dry out, and if the eagle-headed man's eyes dried out he would hold himself personally responsible. But just as Socius Protagynism was about to open his mouth, the eagle-headed man's eyelids slowly came together, first into an elliptical shape, then into a line, then back into an elliptical shape.

Then, suddenly, his hands were on the bag.

Socius Protagynism started. He was beginning to think that the eagle-headed man was not, as he had presupposed, a law enforcer in disguise, judging from the predominantly apathetic countenance he had maintained throughout the course of their encounter. But once those hands placed themselves on the bag, clutched it and removed it from Socius Protagynism's grip, his doubt was overridden and his presupposition was confirmed. He took a step back, to give the eagle-headed man room to work, and said, "Go ahead then. Go ahead. I'm ready."

His deadpan expression persisting, the eagle-headed man finally spoke. "Okay," he murmured in a liquid tone of voice. Then he fumbled for and pinched the tail of the bag's zipper, and jerked it from one side to the other.

"Ah!" exclaimed Socius Protagynism, cowering and paling.

Paying him no attention, the eagle-headed man peered inside . . .

The head lay on the bottom of the bag, looking up at him. It was the size and shape of a human head . . . but it wasn't human. It had the lidless eyes of an octopus and the whiskered mouth of a catfish and the pointy ears of a wolf, and its skin was algae-colored. The cranium of the head was not unlike the eagle-headed man's, sleek and bald. It had no nose. Beneath its flat, wrinkled chin was a gory stump of neck, out of which a fair amount of mucous had poured and dried. This mucous was the color of sky and smelled like hot manure.

Nose twitching like a rabbit's, the eagle-headed man stared at the head. The head stared back at him. He pushed the tip of his tongue between his lips.

"What?" said Socius Protagynism, gesticulating. "What is it?"

The eagle-headed man sucked his cheeks into his mouth as he looked up from the face of the alien in the bag to the face of Socius Protagynism, which was instantly face to face with the alien as the eagle-headed man, avenging himself perhaps, now stuck the bag in his face. At first Socius Protagynism pinched his eyes shut and jerked his head away. But when he heard the eagle-headed man, annoyed by this (he didn't pinch his eyes shut and jerk his head away when the bag was stuck in *his* face), clear his throat, Socius Protagynism forced his eyes to unpinch themselves and turned and faced the open bag.

"I see," said Socius Protagynism and squinted at the head. He squinted at it for a full minute, his lips puckered into a rose-bud that vibrated in a fit of introspection. Anybody paying attention to this fleshy, frenetic rosebud might have thought it was an organism in itself, a living organism discontent with the face it was attached to and struggling in vain to leap off of it, but nobody was paying attention to it (not even the eagle-headed man), and eventually the lips relaxed.

Looking the eagle-headed man in the eyes, Socius Protagynism said, "Guess I overreacted, huh? I just don't like to fly, is all. I'm just nervous, me. Heh heh. Sorry."

The eagle-headed man blinked at him.

Nodding, Socius Protagynism looked down and squinted at the head one more time, to make sure everything was as it should be. It was. So he apologized and thanked the eagle-headed man for being such a good sport, promising never to be inattentive to his carry-on luggage again, and at last he removed the carry-on from the eagle-headed man's grasp, zipped it up and said, "So long!"

Socius Protagynism walked away. He weaved through a gaggle of Hare Krishnas, waited in line, checked his ticket and disappeared through the gate. As he disappeared the thunderhum of the airport diminished considerably, in the ears of the eagle-headed man at least, and for a moment the eagle-headed man wondered if Socius Protagynism's presence had somehow been responsible for intensifying the thunderhum. Perhaps, he speculated, his presence *was* the thunderhum, which was the reason why he had sidled up to the wall in the first place. Whatever the case, the thunderhum had faded into a simple, harmless hum, meaning the traffic on Terminal D's main drag had thinned out and was negotiable. So the eagle-headed man picked up the thin black cane that had fallen onto his feet and, eyelids fluttering over the crystal spheres in his skull, he tap, tap, tap, tap, tapped away . . .

CONVERSATION WITH A HAIR STYLIST

". . . Can you believe they said that to me, my straight-and-narrow cousins? I really don't like my cousins. I could care less if they died, to tell you the truth. Seriously. Anyhow, I'm kind of artsy, kind of a creative spirit. What about *you*? I sense that in you, creativity. I sense everything in everyone. Take my receptionist, for instance. I mean, just take a look at her over there. You think she actually does any *work* around here? I'll tell you something: she doesn't. Oh, she likes to think that I think and that everyone else thinks she works all right, but I know the score, goddman her. What a total loser. Really, when I'm over here at the wash basin, she just sits over there at the front desk with a bitchy look on her fat face and daydreams about her ugly boyfriend. I can see her in the mirror in the corner of the ceiling there, right now I can see her, doing nothing. See her? I get near her, though, and she makes with the scribbling pen and the stressed-out frowns and sighs. You see what I mean? I mean, you know what I'm talking about? That girl. What am I supposed to do with her? What do *you* think I should do? Hell with her, I say. She can go to hell, I say."

The hair stylist utters these words as she lathers up my hair with wintergreen-scented shampoo. But my head is so sharp. My head, beneath my hair, is like a ball of wrapped-up barbed wire. And she soon realizes it. One moment she's brainlessly scrubbing away, the next she realizes that every last one of her fingertips is not only punctured, but maimed. "Ouch!" she chirps. "Ouch! That hurts me, you fiend!" But I'm feeling so comfortable and relaxed now . . . I just can't be bothered. My eyes and ears stay closed, my body stays soft and stationary as, in spite of herself, she finishes the job and rinses my hair out. Then, over on the highchair in front of the mirror, I regard her reflection with simulated concern and say, "I'm sorry." She says nothing. Staring at me slot-eyed, she wiggles her gory fingers at my reflection—blood dribbles onto and stains the long, thin bib I wear—and makes warped shapes with her orange, sun-dried lips. I feel nothing. Still, as if out of duty, I take her hands one at a time and suck hungrily on her fingertips until they've shriveled up like rotten little onion stalks. She farts in ecstasy and thanks me. And strikes up another conversation with herself . . .

ANTIFACE

". . . experiences a sense of Kierkegaardian dread. Neo has the freedom to jack himself back into the matrix at his leisure but he is afraid of that freedom. Why is he afraid of that freedom? Because of his recently acquired knowledge of it, of course. Thus we are faced with a power-knowledge structure that operates, in Foucault's words, as a (quote) matrix of transformation (unquote). The pun on matrix here is in need of some attention, but we will come back to it in due course. For now, let's turn to the aforementioned clip in which Neo is about to discover, in Gibson's words now, the (quote) consensual hallucination that is the matrix (unquote) for the first time. Neo has just taken a pill that will disrupt his input-output signal and switch his sensory perception from matrix-spacetime to real-spacetime. He is sitting in a chair with various trodes attached to his extremities. Next to him is a cracked mirror—and mirrors, as we know, often signify schizophrenia in film, especially if they are cracked. At any rate Neo fixes his gaze on the mirror and looks on as the cracks collapse in upon themselves and disappear, rendering the mirror perfectly smooth. Pay special attention to the expression on the reflection of Neo's face. Also note the manner in which the expression fluctuates after Neo sticks his finger into the mirror, which has become aqueous."

Visiting Professor Paynstake bends over and begins fumbling with the VCR sitting on a little chair next to the television. One by one he pushes all of the buttons on the control panel, but none of them seem to be the right one, so he starts pushing with more enthusiasm. "This fucking thing," he mumbles. He mumbles some more things and the more he mumbles the more his profound belly jiggles and heaves and rolls and sways back and forth . . .

It is not long before the back of Visiting Professor Paynstake's dress shirt comes loose and exposes the tip of an ass crack. Out of the ass crack shoots an angry tuft of gray hair.

A few of the professors and graduate students that have been listening to Visiting Professor Paynstake's paper wince at this virtually scatological display, but most of them remain plain-faced and overlook it since the paper has turned out to be interesting enough so far, if for nothing else than the paper is a theoretically-oriented analysis of a kung-fu science fiction film. Graduate Student Deviation, on the other hand, neither winces nor remains plain-faced. He doesn't grimace either, nor does he scowl or frown. Instead he makes a face that might best be described as an antiface, a face that is undoubtedly a face, yes, but that is also not a face at all, is so far from being a face that it is absurd to even speak or think the word "face" in its immediate presence. And when Graduate Student Deviation makes this antiface, Full Professor O'Darkness, the chair of Pseudofolliculitis State University's English department and the spitting image of Henry David Thoreau (albeit Full Professor O'Darkness is a good foot and a half taller than the lilliputian Thoreau and has the physique of Schwarzenegger in his muscular prime), spots him right away. His stony face turns purple with fury, his nostrils flare to the size of half dollars, veins pop out of his skin in droves. He springs to his feet like a hoe that's been stepped on. Eyes round as golf balls, he raises an arm and extends a rage-filled finger.

"You, sir!" he says. "YOU!!!"

The lecture hall in which Visiting Professor Paynstake is presenting his paper is not big. It has a fifty person capacity but there are only about thirty professors and graduate students in attendance, and when Full Professor O'Darkness, standing in the front row, points his finger at and accuses Graduate Student Deviation, sitting in the back row, everybody immediately turns around and glues their eyes to the accused, except Visiting Professor Paynstake. Visiting Professor Paynstake is so preoccupied by his failure to negotiate the VCR he hears nothing but the sound of his own obscene muttering.

When Graduate Student Deviation's fellow graduate students see that he is making an antiface, most of them blush and begin fidgeting uncomfortably in their seats, and Graduate Students Hiddenlip and Frood urinate in their pants, and Graduate Student Realthing implodes in shame.

When Full Professor O'Darkness's fellow professors see that Graduate Student Deviation is making an antiface, most of them go white in the face and rigid as tree stumps in their seats, and Associate Professors Kulminate and Blinkman stand and mimic Full Professor O'Darkness's indicting posture, and Assistant Professor Zarathustra, following in Graduate Student Realthing's footsteps (and well aware of the irony of a professor following in a graduate student's footsteps), implodes in shame.

"Young man," continues Full Professor O'Darkness, "you are embarrassing us in front of Visiting Professor Paynstake. Embarrassing us! Granted, the man has clearly exposed himself to us in a less than becoming fashion. Yes, *there* is an ass crack"—he points at it—"and yes, *there* is a disgusting-looking tuft of hair sticking out of that ass crack"—points at it—"but that is no reason for you"—pointing at Graduate Student Deviation again—"to lose your composure. Control yourself! I don't care if Visiting Professor Paynstake drops his trousers, moons us and a groundhog leaps out of his backside, this is no way to react! Put that away, sir. I say, put that antiface away before I come over there and put it away for you. You are denigrating the good name of this English department—nay, of this entire institution! Do you hear me Graduate Student Deviation? Graduate Student Deviation—I implore you to desist!"

Graduate Student Deviation—does not desist. He continues to make his antiface.

Oblivious to Full Professor O'Darkness's invective, and to Graduate Student Deviation's antiface, and to everybody's reaction to Graduate Student Deviation's antiface, Visiting Professor Paynstake picks up the VCR and begins strangling it. It is a pathetic display but at least, when he stands erect, his ass is concealed by the crinkled tail of his dress shirt.

And yet Graduate Student Deviation goes on making an antiface. Why? wonders Full Professor O'Darkness, lowering his finger but remaining purple-faced and flared in the nostrils (Associate Professors Kulminate and Blinkman do the same). Is he mad? Everybody's looking at him, everybody's clearly embarrassed for and by him. Does that please him? Does he take some kind of sadistic pleasure in embarrassing people? Does he take some kind of masochistic pleasure in embarrassing himself? Perhaps he's sadomasochistic in that he enjoys embarrassing other people while at the same time embarrassing himself. Or perhaps he's not embarrassed at all. Does this graduate student have the psychological stamina to make a fool out of himself in public and feel nothing, nothing at all? I envy him if that's the case. But whatever the case, whether he's embarrassed or not—is this a simple matter of cause and effect, or does Graduate Student Deviation have a conscious motive? Was the sudden emergence of this antiface a direct result of the sudden emergence of Professor Paynstake's exposed ass and ass hair or was the emergence of the antiface premeditated? That is to say, did Graduate Student Deviation plan to come in here this afternoon and at some point or another make that antiface? If so, why? To undermine my authority? To make me look like a total idiot in front of Visiting Professor Paynstake, who will no doubt return to his home institution, the University of Tetracycline, and say to his colleagues there, "Full Professor O'Darkness is a total idiot!" Why would Graduate Student Deviation want to do that to me? I don't even know Graduate Student Deviation very well. In fact, I've only had one conversation with him, on the phone, before he had even applied to the English graduate program here at Pseudofolliculitis State. Does he resent me for not having another phone conversation since then? What does he expect me to do, call him on the phone all the time? If only I had rejected his application! But I didn't reject him, I accepted him. And now he's making me pay for it. The thanks I get. I'm never accepting another graduate student into this program again, no matter how well they score on the G.R.E. *Never . . .*

Little does Full Professor O'Darkness know that Graduate Student Deviation's antiface has nothing to do with Visiting Professor Paynstake's crass exhibition.

The thing is, Graduate Student Deviation, who as a graduate student is required to attend roughly eight visiting professor paper presentations a semester, has grave difficulty concentrating on orally transmitted pieces of critical writing. No matter how provocative, engaging and lucid the subject matter, despite his efforts he just can't keep his mind from wandering. Typically his mind begins to wander after this or that presenter has read the first few sentences of his or her paper, and while he fights the urge to give in to his mind, by the third page of the paper he is almost always occupied by an intense daydream. The intensity of this afternoon's daydream was, for reasons unknown to Graduate Student Deviation, unlike any he had had before, and the only way his body knew how to respond to the daydream was by making an antiface. It just so happened that the emergence of the antiface coincided with the emergence of Visiting Professor Paynstake's ass hair—the event was pure coincidence. Moreover, Graduate Student Deviation was so captivated by the intensity of his daydream, his antiface persisted throughout the course of Full Professor O'Darkness's invective, which he didn't hear or see, and the antiface is still going strong right now. But Full Professor O'Darkness, or anybody else for that matter, have no way of knowing Graduate Student Deviation is having the daydream to end all daydreams. Nobody can blame Full Professor O'Darkness for wanting to destroy this antiface maker. For all he knows, Graduate Student Deviation is out to get him. "And he who is out to get me," seethes Full Professor O'Darkness, "is going to get me all right. He's going to get me like a motherfuckin FREIGHT TRAIN!!!"

Full Professor O'Darkness is about to leap across the lecture hall, tackle Graduate Student Deviation and hammer his antiface back into a normal face. But just as he clenches his fists and squats, Graduate Student Deviation's daydream unexpectedly and abruptly decreases in intensity, like a sprinter that in mid-sprint steps in a hole in the ground and twists his ankle, and so Graduate Student Deviation's antiface disappears, dissolves back into a normal face—just as Visiting Professor Paynstake, by means of strangulation, manages to get the VCR to play! Another amazing coincidence. And as Visiting Professor Paynstake places the VCR back down on its chair, Full Professor O'Darkness, still paranoid, still incensed, still pulsing with veins, but in control of himself, forces himself back into his seat, and Associate Professors Kulminate and Blinkman, as always, follow his lead. Then, in one smooth motion, everybody (except the recently imploded Assistant Professor Zarathustra and Graduate Student Realthing of course) rotates their necks and their gazes shift from Graduate Student Deviation's now blank, ordinary, anesthetized-looking face to Visiting Professor Paynstake—who, making a face, says, "Don't look at me! Look at the damn clip, you monkies!"

THE WIENER DOG ON THE CEILING

One night my friend Herman got himself pregnant. Herman's a hermaphrodite, and it wasn't the first time something like this happened. He's always getting himself pregnant, actually, and this time he went to the hospital and gave birth to twins, one girl and one hermaphrodite. After taking a nap, he put some diapers on them. Then he came over to my place.

I was lying naked on my couch with my arms folded behind my head. A daddy long legs was on my ceiling. How did it get in here? There were no crannies in the walls of my house that it could have squeezed itself through. I knew this because I checked the walls every morning, after breakfast, to reassure myself.

"Good evening," Herman intoned. He nodded politely at me.

I didn't reply, didn't even acknowledge his presence. Too busy thinking about the spider.

The twins tucked beneath his arms, Herman tip-toed over to the couch and dropped the twins onto my chest. They wiggled uncomfortably. They started bawling. I wiped them off of me with the back of a hand as the spider scrambled into a light bulb and went up in a little puff of smoke. I knew it saw the light bulb, it having plenty of eyes, but I wondered if it knew that the light bulb would kill it, that is, I wondered if the spider committed suicide.

Herman picked the twins up by the ankles. His hermaphrodite's diaper came loose and hit the floor with a splat. Herman left it there. He put the twins on my chest again.

I wiped them off again. Sighed. The ceiling was depressing.

Herman scooped up the twins. Tossed them on my chest now. I went "Oof!" when they hit me, then looked down at them. They were slick with tears and growing slicker by the moment. Their cries were the epitome of pain.

"Stop doing that," I said. I took a deep breath. My chest puffed up and the twins toppled onto the floor.

"No," said Herman.

"No?" In my periphery I noticed another bug on the ceiling. No, it wasn't a bug. It was a dog. One of those wiener things. How did *it* get in here? I made a pact with myself to be more attentive to my walls. I would have to start checking them after lunch and dinner, too.

"Yes. *No*." Herman puckered up his lips. He collected the twins, put them on my chest. "I'm not ready to stop yet," he shrugged. "Only when I'm ready to stop will I stop doing what I'm doing. I probably won't stop for a while. I probably won't stop until I get so tired I just fall asleep standing here. Have you ever fallen asleep standing somewhere? Better yet, have you ever fallen asleep while you were walking down the street? I have. I fell asleep on my way over here, if you want to know the truth. I'm not even narcoleptic. Not a diagnosed narcoleptic anyhow. Anyhow when I hit the asphalt the twins did too. They cried. People walked by us and scratched themselves. Then I woke up and rocked the twins until they stopped crying and snuck in here, through your front door. It was wide open. Well, here I am. And here are the twins. And I'm not going to stop showing them to you until I fall asleep again. I don't know when that might happen. Maybe in a minute, maybe not for a couple of days. Maybe never, goddamn you. What do you think about that?"

Filtering out the wet, squirming agony of the flesh on my flesh, I turned my attention to the upside-down wiener dog.

A few minutes passed before I said, "Do whatever you have to do."

After the dog circumvented the light bulb, it moved forward like a snail and, like a snail, left a gooey substance in its train.

MY MOTHER'S PILLOWS

"Welcome, welcome," I said to the person on my doorstep. He was wearing a fetus-flesh trench coat on his body and a piece of concrete on his head. I had never seen him before. The person was a total stranger, and his name, unless the leather tag sewed onto his left eyeball wasn't telling the truth, was Mr. Plip. "I've been waiting for you," I lied, to make him feel wanted. I have a problem with wanting to make people feel wanted. "Please, sir! Come in!"

After hyperexamining me and then the terrain behind each of his moist, puffed-up shoulders, Mr. Plip nodded and stepped into my foyer . . . and proceeded to wipe the cow manure on the soles of his galoshes onto my welcome mat. That's when I realized I had made a mistake, but it was too late now: he was in. All I could do was try to make the best of it. And, despite my soiled welcome mat, maybe, just maybe, I hadn't made a mistake after all! I would have to wait and see.

"May I take your coat and ha—"

Before I could finish he tipped his head down and the piece of concrete slid off of him and onto my hardwood floor, cracking it wide open. The trench coat came off, then, was balled up and deposited in the crack. It all happened very fast.

Save the galoshes on his feet and the name tag on his eyeball, Mr. Plip was naked. He was as skinny and hairy as a water rat.

"Uhm," I managed as he whisked past me and into my lounge. There he flopped his bony ass down onto the only article of furniture available to him, a long Naugahyde couch, and picked up one of the little hand-nit pillows that my mother had made for me. There were a dozen or so of them scattered across the couch. They were all about the same size, but they varied in color and shape, and the one Mr. Plip had selected was a green square, or diamond, depending upon how you looked at it. I had grown attached to these pillows over the years and when I walked into my lounge and over to the couch, I felt the flame of nausea kindle in my stomach as Mr. Plip first began squishing the pillow in his hands, then licking it. I dry-heaved when he began rubbing it all over his chest and arms, as if it might be a bar of soap.

"Mr. Plip," I said, towering over him. I stood in front of the couch like a marine at attention. "Would you mind leaving that pillow alone please? I'd certainly appreciate it. I think in the long run you'd appreciate it, too. What do you say? Do we have a deal or no?"

I didn't expect him to listen to me—I never expect anybody to listen to me—so I was a bit surprised when he stopped rubbing himself and looked up at me. He even set the pillow down beside him on the couch, although he continued to squish it a little with his thumb and index finger. Still, I was hopeful. Maybe this one would do the right thing. There was no reason for him to do the right thing; after all, I had invited him into my space without even knowing how he acted in his own space. So, whatever he did, to my pillow, to my couch, to my hardwood floor, to me . . . I deserved it. And yet I couldn't help but think that this one would be the one that came around!

He wasn't. Before I could so much as blink he had taken up the pillow again and buried it in the brambly black tuft of his groin. Then the doorbell rang again and I was compelled to stand and usher Mr. Plip into the corner of my lounge where he yanked the pillow out of his groin and, along with the rest of the people there, each of which had one of my mother's pillows in hand, squished it, and licked it, and squished it some more.

LOOK'D TOO NEAR

Glories, like glow-worms, afar off shine bright,
But look'd too near, have neither heat nor light.

— John Webster, *The Duchess of Malfi*

I grabbed hold of the knob and twisted it, and pulled.

Beyond the door I met an outsider. He was, in all respects, an extraordinary specimen. I double-taked him, despite how I felt about the kind of people that double-taked, but I was helpless to the human instinct to double-take when an extraordinary specimen comes along, so I did it. Then I just looked at him for a minute or two.

He was a sort of Adonis, this outsider, in my opinion at least—one human's Adonis may be another's Caliban—and I had to bite my lip to keep from crying out. He stood there in the crackling neon of the corridor, staring at me and giving me chills.

He was built like a comic book superhero. His smooth, smooth skin was the color of maple leaves. His emerald green eyes and his physique, especially his pectoral and abdominal muscles, were exquisite. He was not too tall, wore his hair not too long, had not too big genitals, and the expression on his aquiline face, if I was reading it correctly, was friendly—but not too friendly; there was a hint of standoffishness in his expression as well, and my gut reaction was that this was his normal expression, which I found abnormal, most people being either too friendly or too standoffish. Anyway, he was a real treat!

"Your abdomen is like the backside of an armadillo," I

said and broke the ice. "I must shake your hand. And I will."
Sticking out my hand, I moved towards him.

He backed away. We were about twenty feet apart and he seemed determined to keep that distance between us.

"Stay where you are," he insisted.

"Why? I just want to shake your hand." To assure him that I was telling the truth, I pointed at my outstretched hand with the hand that had, just a moment ago, been hiding behind my back. I also gave him the most sociable grin in my grinning repertoire.

The outsider wouldn't take the bait. I took one step towards him, he took one step backwards. Was it because I double-taked him? Possibly. "You're not angry with me, are you?" I asked.

"Stay back! Stay back!" He punched out at the air in front of him with his fists a few times, as if the force of the blows might somehow reach me and keep me in check, maybe knock me unconscious.

I took three more steps forward. The outsider took three more steps backwards. Finally I stopped. Shrugged. "I'll leave the ball in your court," I said to him. "When you feel ready to come over and shake my hand, I'll be here. Take your time."

We stared at each other.

It took a little while, longer than I thought it would, but eventually the outsider caved. It was a kind of pathetic process. At first he stared at me straight-backed, with his arms akimbo, his chin up, flexing every single muscle strand in his body that he had the power to flex. I, too, stared at him straight-backed, but I let my arms hang freely at my sides, and my chin was neither up nor down, was exactly where it should have been, and I made no effort to flex any muscles seeing as my nakedness was concealed by a trenchcoat. Anyway it started with the outsider's chin, which drooped, slowly, very slowly, until it ran into his clavicle bone, at which point his back had seemed to develop a hunch, and his arms to have died: they dangled there like two lynched things. Also, his musculature, while still impressive, was no longer strained.

"That's it," I said reassuringly, "don't be afraid. I'm not going to hurt you. As I said, a handshake is all I require. You have my word. One handshake, with no more than five pumps. Then I'll be on my way."

As he narrowed the gap between us with delicate baby-steps, the outsider made an attempt to respond to me, but all that came out of his mouth were these goofy croaking noises. I couldn't help but smile. My smile grew wider with each croak, until I was sporting a full blown rictus grin . . . which, once the outsider was about ten feet away from me, deflated into an appalled smirk . . .

I wanted to tell him to stop, to turn around and go away. I wanted to take hold of the knob and twist it and pull and get out of the corridor, go back inside, where I belonged. But there was no going back now. Once I start something I always finish it, no matter how it turns out. I had coerced this outsider, if only by my presence and my looks, into approaching me and shaking my hand, and if I didn't oblige him, I wouldn't be able to live with myself. I had to follow through, there was no other option —to not follow through would be to not be me.

I noticed the first change when the outsider narrowed the gap between us to eight feet and all of his hair fell out, as if the hair had not been connected to his head at all but was just lying there, and a strong gust of wind came along and blew it away.

At seven feet, liver spots popped up everywhere on him. All over his body there were liver spots now. Or were those scales?

At six feet his arms, legs and groin were consumed by

varicose veins that squiggled like live things. "Are you okay?" I managed to squeak out. No answer. He kept on coming.

When the outsider was five feet away his nose and ears fell off. Four feet and there went his lips and the lips struck the floor with a tiny splat and, like the nose and ears, decayed into nothingness before my eyes. By the time he was three feet from me, what remained of his flesh had gone up in smoke, leaving only a gray-boned skeleton with eyeballs and a flailing tongue behind.

At two feet the eyeballs and the tongue came out. And his bones became bone meal. And the bone meal crumbled to the floor and, not one foot from my toes, became a big pile of manure. Wide-eyed, I looked down at the manure, hoping it would crawl away. It didn't. It stayed right where it was, quivering a bit, and I frowned at the outsider as a thick brown strand extended out of its bulk, sluggishly, like a worm burrowing out of a tough-skinned apple. Initially the end of the strand was smoothly rounded. Then it developed five little brown strands of its own, and soon it resembled an everyday ordinary old hand . . . except that this hand, unlike most others, was made of shit.

Serves me right, I told myself. You should have just minded your own business. You should have just left him alone. Why can't you just mind your own business, and leave people alone? You know what happens if you don't. You get closer to them. You get to know them. And then . . .

I shook my head.

Then, taking a deep breath, I kept my word. I shook the hand.

THE TRUTH ABOUT HUMPTY DUMPTY

People that get all bent out of shape when they hear about what happened to Humpty Dumpty really put me in a bad mood. My wife, for example, every time she hears about it, can't stop blubbering over that goddamn egg. "Poor old Humpty," she'll say to me with a long glassy-eyed sigh. "If only he hadn't sat on that wall!" Then she'll sigh some more, shake her head, pace up and down the stairs a bit, maybe cry, maybe take a Valium, maybe go lock herself in the bathroom or go outside and dig gopher holes in the back yard. I used to tell her she was too emotional. She used to tell me I was too unemotional. Once, she said, "You're as unemotional as a pile of bloody testicles quivering in the wind!" I didn't entirely understand what she meant by that but it wasn't an image that my mind's screen enjoyed having plastered on it. So afterwards, whenever my wife heard the story of Humpty Dumpty—sometimes she reads it, sometimes one of her girlfriends comes over and whispers it into her ear (they sob in each other's arms afterwards), sometimes she just tells the story to her reflection in the mirror—I kept my mouth shut and let her rant. If she only knew that Humpty Dumpty hadn't been the luckless, easy-going gentleman that she made him out to be! If she only knew that Humpty Dumpty had been a drunk, a whore lover, a shoplifter and a grandmother sniffer! If she only knew that all the king's horses and all the king's men forced him to sit on the wall and then blew on him until he fell off, putting an end to his village idiocy once and for all! If she only knew that that insane egg's last burping words, as his rotund yoke leaked out of him, had been, "I shall come back from the dead and satanize every last one of you fuckin assholes!" If she knew these things, as I do, my wife might not act like such a baby, and I might not be in such a bad mood all the time.

But she doesn't know them. And despite myself, telling her about them has never crossed my mind.

EROTIC POEM

"The ultimate condition of production
is the reproduction of the conditions of production."

—Louis Althusser, "Ideology and Ideological State Apparatuses"

The audience consists of movie stars that have slipped off their skin, turned the skin inside out and put it back on. The smell of the undersides of all these skins is tantamount to and as unbearable as the innards of a dump truck yet nobody seems to recognize it. Not even the professional entertainer.

On stage Jackson Donne, the professional entertainer, is in the middle of his routine. There is a candystriped pillar rising out of the stage and Jackson Donne is playing hide and seek with himself. One moment he will hide behind the pillar so that nobody can see him—curiously, the pillar is thin as a flagpole and everybody can see him—the next he will hop out into the open. Turning to the pillar and pointing behind it, he'll say, "Ah ha!" Nobody's there, of course, so he says, "Damnit!" and hides behind the pillar again, and jumps out into the open again. "Ah ha!" he says, then, "Damnit!" and then he hides behind the pillar and starts over, determined to catch himself in the act of hiding. This part of the routine goes on for over thirty minutes. Then Jackson Donne gets tired and frustrated and at last suicidal.

Well. Move on to the next part of the routine.

But what is the next part of his routine? He can't remember. Because he has stagefright? No, he doesn't get stagefright. Does he? He can't remember. Probably because he has stagefright. Then again, maybe him not rembering he has stagefright because he has stagefright is part of the routine. He decides to ask a member of the audience.

"Do I have stagefright? I'm asking you, sir."

With cold eyes and pointing index finger he is addressing a male in the front row who might be Tom Cruise or Brad Pitt or Mel Gibson or Sean Penn or Antonio Banderas or any other short slight movie star—everybody looks more or less the same when their skin is on backwards, after all. But whoever it is is being subtley yet effectively molested by the female— Gwenyth Paltrow? Sandra Bullock? Winnona Ryder?—sitting next to him and he doesn't respond to Jackson Donne with so much as a nod or a headshake let alone a polite yes or no. He doesn't even screw up his hideous face.

"Asshole!" says Jackson Donne as his hairtrigger temper detonates and he stagedives onto the movie star and begins pounding in his moist red head. Eventually the head pops off and each member of the audience's mouth crinkles into a pensive anus shape. Jackson Donne takes a loud bow. Then he does a highflying backflip back onto the stage and takes another bow as frantic waiters appear out of nowhere passing out hors d'oeuvres and martinis and little sandwich bags full of *Bannisteria caapit* and when they run out of things to pass out they are assimilated into the gaping flesh of the audience with screams that fade into whimpers that fade into . . .

Sound of chirping crickets and frogs. Then silence.

"The monstrous silence of modernity!" yowls Jackson Donne and pretends a mosquito lands on his cheek and starts sucking on him. He nails himself in the face with a ham fist. He hits the stage like a block of concrete, legs in the air. He gets up and bows . . . and remembers the next part of his routine: bow, deeply, over and over again, until he passes out.

. . . like a block of concrete . . .

When Jackson Donne wakes up he keeps his eyes closed

and his body still. Only pretending to be passed out now. He listens to the audience's throat-clearings and nose-blowings and wonders, number one, if Al Pacino is in the audience, and number two, if Al Pacino is flexing his jaw at him. Then he pretends to be jarred awake from a nightmare. His scream is so loud and powerful that his Adam's apple flies out of his throat and brains a movie star in the third row. After hopping off the stage and retrieving the Adam's apple, and swallowing it back into place, Jackson Donne hops back on stage and faces the audience. Positioning his left heel against the left flank of his right foot, throwing back his shoulders, throwing up his chin, he proceeds to stare at the audience, with eyes that are frowning and bulging at the same time, for two hours. During this period a few small, relatively tame orgies materialize here and there but none of them last very long and for the most part the audience members are still, silent, and staring back at him. Then a terribly obese movie star that is in all likelihood Marlon Brando stands and drops his pants and starts pissing in the aisle. He sighs like dull thunder.

Jackson Donne blurts, "Knock that shit off, you!" and the movie star, stiffening up, nervously pinches his fleshy, blood-covered penis and sits back down with a great squeak of chair. "Can't you see I'm busy up here?"

The routine resumes. Jackson Donne reads the first volume of Karl Marx's *Capital* aloud, then reads the fragmented entirety of Walter Benjamin's *Passagen-Werk* to himself. Then he plucks out every single hair in his left nostril without sneezing once. "OUCH!!!" he exclaims with each horrible pluck. Then he says, "And now I shall read you an erotic poem. The poem is called 'Erotic Poem' and reads:

The vast genital
dangling

from the ceiling
snaps and
falls on my head
like a chandelier
in the wet moonlight."

This said, Jackson Donne lifts up his shirt and exposes two screaming assholes where his nipples are supposed to be. Then he juggles a flock of screaming shrunken heads. Then he oils up and flexes his tricep muscles. Then he stuffs his fingers in his mouth, whistles, and a jungle stampede of circus freaks scurries on and off stage, excecuting ungainly dance moves. Then he pulls the grinning skeleton of James Dean out of a hat and crucifies it on a rotten wooden cross that he also pulls out of the hat. Then he vomits a small child into a paper cup. Then he murders the first two rows of the audience, one movie star at a time, with select martial arts weapons. Then, tired, frustrated, cramped up, overheated, sweaty, dirty, livid, and bored mindless—Jackson Donne throws in the towel. As usual, his routine has generated few if any emotional responses in the audience and so, as usual, he strips naked and waves his bleached white underwear back and forth over his head, saying, "I surrender you sunzabitches. I give up!" But even saying this doesn't generate a response. If, in their pathological apathy, they're not carressing or fucking one another, the members of the audience remain seated, and still, and silent, and staring at him, and finally Jackson Donne, nodding in dark understanding, is compelled to do that which he is compelled to do at the end of every night: slip off his skin . . . turn the skin inside out . . . put the skin back on . . .

"Only thing keeps you bastards coming back for more!" he booms, extending his arms as the standing ovation escalates in intensity.

THE CAPE

Once we concluded that walking into the funhouse would not be the most reasonable thing to do, my sibling and I walked into the funhouse. "Welcome to the funhouse!" said the Master of Cerebellums, bowing. He bowed so deeply and powerfully his head flew through his open legs and swung up over his rear. He stayed that way for a moment, smirking at us, looking like he had stuffed his torso into the pockets of his pants. Then he unraveled himself, took each of us by the hand and ushered us over to the ladder. The funhouse was as spacious as a small metropolis and the ladder was in the very middle of it. In addition to the three of us, it was the funhouse's only fixture.

"En haut!" spat the MC in French, gesticulating at the ladder. "Haut! Haut!" My sibling and I blinked at each other. The MC made a face at us, then swept himself up in his cape and the cape fell to the earth in a clump, empty.

"He's gone," I whispered out a mouth corner. My sibling nodded disinterestedly.

Sighing, I gripped the ladder to test its sturdiness. It seemed pretty sturdy to me. My sibling gripped it and disagreed, but I pointed out that she had gripped one pole of the ladder and I had gripped the other, and if one pole is sturdy, they all are. "One strong thing is strong enough for everything," I said. Again my sibling disagreed, claiming, "One weak thing is weak enough to kill." I asked her why she always had to play the devil's advocate. She said she wasn't playing the devil's advocate, she genuinely believed in the assertion she had made. "I believe in all of the assertions I make," she insisted. "That doesn't mean you're not in cahoots with the devil," I smirked. She stuck her tongue out at at me. I grabbed the tongue and, pretending it was a weed, yanked it out of her mouth and threw it on the ground and stomped on it. She frowned at me. She picked the tongue up and pet it like a wounded cat, then popped it back in her mouth. "Well?" she said. "Let's go already."

I went first. My sibling followed close at my heels. Now and then during the climb she pinched my Achilles tendons, sometimes playfully, tickling them, sometimes painfully, digging into them with her nails. The ladder was a few miles high so it took us a few hours to get to the top. At the top was a little platform and when we got there I thrust a finger in my sibling's face and said, "You see? You see?" Then I started to do a war dance. A war dance of victory. My sibling told me to stop, but I didn't. I kept on war dancing, even though my Achilles tendons were raining blood all over the funhouse.

And in no time at all the platform, which was thin and brittle as a graham cracker, split open and my sibling and I were heading for ground zero at hundreds of mph. I swore all the way. My sibling swore, too, at me and at life in general, but then, as we were nearing the end, she stopped. "Why aren't you swearing anymore!" I screamed over the scream of the wind. My sibling shrugged. I was about to ask her if the shrug meant she didn't know why she had stopped swearing, or if it meant it didn't matter whether she was swearing or not, when she reached into her pants and pulled the Master of Cerebellum's cape out of them. Evidently she had stashed it in there and snuck it up the ladder with us, for whatever reason (my sibling's logic is more or less a mystery to me), and now she unfurled the flapping thing and, in one fluid motion, swept us both up in it.

The cape smelled funny. It smelled like so much cheap perfume splashed all over a wild animal's ass. I wanted to tell my sibling to get rid of it, get me out of this thing before its stink drowns me. But before I had a chance the cape was laying there on the earth in a clump, empty.

THE BOOK

"Better to be the village idiot than to drown in a sea of hot shit!"

—Socrates as he streaked naked and drunk across
the floor of the colloseum during a political forum.

"Now doan open that book now, boy," twanged the old redneck, pointing a vicious index finger, "I seen that thar book before. I'm warnin yi now!" He thrust the golf ball-sized lump in his underlip at me and threatened to use my face as a spittoon.

I nodded. Then I opened the book, neglecting to read its cover or spine out of sheer spite, and dodged the tobacco-stained spitball discharged from the bearded lips of my ignorant, uninvited guest. But when I tried to read the book I found myself at a loss: there were no words on the pages. There weren't even any pages. There was just this big black hole in the middle of the binding out of which a powerful geyser of shit erupted, blinding me.

"What's the name of that book!" I gurgle-barked at the redneck, who said, "*Tolja* so, boy," and disappeared through a trap door with a snigger.

I tried with frantic, adrenalized hands to close the book— but once opened, I suddenly understood, it could not be escaped. And in any case the book was soon out of reach, and I was soon entirely immersed in its void, which filled my home from floor to ceiling, wall to wall, insulating the quickly rotting yoke that was my body.

STORY ON THE SPHERE

Everything was progressing nicely, I was performing better than ever, until the major-domo and his three henchmen, all of them dressed up in white tuxedos and handlebar mustaches, rolled the sphere into the dining room, at which point the young lady in whose ear I had been whispering pulled back and, her lips tightening into a bloodless sphincter, smacked me across left cheek, then right cheek, with a long rawhide glove. As the lady, whose name I had not yet come to know, or cared to know (names mean nothing to me, nothing at all), awkwardly click-clacked away in her high heels into the arms of another clean-shaven, gracile male, who consoled her by playing with one of her exposed nipples, the rest of the guests burst out into laughter, pointing back and forth at me and the sphere that was now standing in front of my toes. The sphere came up to my knees and was perhaps the size of a Chinese soccer ball; judging by the sound it made when it was rolled across the hardwood floor and the barreling manner with which it had gained headway, the weight of it was immense; and glued to the surface of the sphere, by means of rubber cement if my nose wasn't failing me, was a story of mine, the entire manuscript of "Story on the Sphere," which I had written upstairs, in my royal suite, the night before. Stunned, I rattled my head. Was I dreaming? If not, what was the meaning of this? If so—what was the meaning of this?

"How dare you, sir," I ejaculated, feeling violated, whatever the reality of my circumstances. But the major-domo just went on sniggering along with everybody else, save a handful of blue-haired couples that, having read a page or two from off the sphere, cast gazes like cracking whips in my direction or abused me with hard gestures or words. My lady friend, in contrast, had disrobed and begun having sex with her new partner on the dance floor, under a spinning disco ball, and was completely apathetic; she could have cared less about me, or my story, or the fact that the major-domo had, for some reason, presumably broken into my suite, taken my manuscript and plastered it all over this sphere. I called her a name out of the corner of my mouth. Then, to the major-domo: "Get this out of here at once." I gesticulated at the sphere as if it might have been a rotten, stinking cadaver. "I could have you arrested. And I should. Go on now, get it out. This has no business here. This hasn't even been properly revised. Take it out. Roll it away. Back to my room, where you stole it from." I widened my eyes and bore my teeth at the major-domo, imploring him to do the right thing. At that one of his henchmen snapped his teeth into a dirty yellow grin that matched the bow tie and cummerbund of his tuxedo, and the other two henchmen did likewise, with the same matching grins. The diminutive, pencil-faced major-domo folded his hands behind his back. "I'm very sorry, sir," he said with a smug accent, "but I must politely decline. You wrote it, you roll it away."

Horrified, I stared at the sphere, read some of my words . . . Covering my mouth, I burped. Vertigo and then nausea overwhelmed me and I vomited all over a passing cocktail waitress that was carrying a platter of hors d'oeuvres. The platter fell to the floor with a splash of egg yolks, artichoke hearts, caviar clusters, frog legs. The waitress fell on top of the rubble. She sat there spread-legged, a dazed, almost uninterested look on her face, which bore a hideous mask of noxious vomit.

In seconds the dining room cleared, its unnerved occupants pinching their lips and noses shut as they made for the doors like a herd of mad cows. "Seize him!" screamed the major-domo, holding his ground. The smell and the sight of the vomit, however, prompted him to reach into a hidden pocket and draw out a giant clothes pin. Quickly, but at the same time very carefully, he applied this to his head, with two hands, as if putting on a crown. When he released his hands and let them drop to his sides, his face was squeezed out of sight, except for the handlebars of his mustache and his lips; and because of the pressure exerted by the clothes pin's forks, the lips puffed out like sausages and turned purple. "Seize him!" the lips screamed again, mousily this time. But the major-domo's sidekicks were gone. Save the benumbed, soiled waitress and the two cooing lovers on the dance floor it was only he and I now, he and I and the sphere, which somehow I had managed to lift up, and with my hands to compress down to the size of a baseball, albeit the thing weighed a good three hundred pounds. But I'm actually quite strong, and here I was made stronger by my excited, adrenalized state, so I had no trouble winding up and hurling the sphere straight through the major-domo, who could of course not see to duck out of the way. Well, it was a bullseye. As black blood and organs poured out of the big hole in his chest, the major-domo ran around like a headless chicken, and he even made chicken wing motions with his arms, but then he tripped on a ripple in the carpet, tumbled over and, following substantial twitching and one all-out seizure, lay still.

Later, after I calmed down and was completely alone— the lovers eventually grew bored and crawled away—I went looking for the sphere. I found it underneath a table. I got down on my knees, pushed aside a chair and crawled over to it, to see if I might salvage "Story on the Sphere," the only copy being this hand-written one here. But the lettering was too small now; I couldn't read it; when I compressed the sphere, I also compressed the matter attached to it. What could I do? The story was in awful shape. It was embarrassingly put together and in dire need of revision, like all of my writing, all of it. Nonetheless the idea behind the story was perhaps the best one I had ever come up with. Only, I had forgotten the idea. And not twenty-four hours had passed me by since it was fresh in my head. It was gone, though, totally gone, not a trace of it remained. Did it have something to do with a disagreeable man and his disagreeable sidekicks plastering an innocent man's story all over a giant sphere and then rolling the sphere out of the private and into the public arena? Maybe. Probably. Why else would the major-domo have done what he did? But again, I had forgotten the idea. I had no idea what the idea had to do with.

On hands and knees I frowned at the sphere for a long time, frowned and squinted at the tangled maze of black lines that circumscribed it. At last I let my buttocks fall back on my heels. Ducking down a bit, so as not to bump my head into the underside of the table, I opened my hands as wide as possible and grabbed hold of my head, and tried to compress it down to a size that would be proportionate with the size of the sphere, so that I might read and refamiliarize myself with "Story on the Sphere."

But I only succeeded in giving myself a headache. It hurt so much, I tossed and turned all night.

HOGAN MARSUPIAL

I

And like Jay Gatsby's lapdog Nick Carroway, Hogan Marsupial considered the midwest, where he was born and raised, to be "the ragged edge of the universe," so as soon as he graduated from Pseudofolliculitis State University, a small private college in Ohio, he moved out west to Hollywood, another ragged edge of the universe, far more ragged than the midwest, "but it least it doesn't snow out here," Marsupial told his parents in his defense, "and I prefer the company of rappers and movie stars to grocery store clerks anyhow. No offense." This preference didn't stop Marsupial from getting a job as a grocery store clerk once he settled into a cruddy, roach-infested studio apartment on Dean Drive, but his father owned a grocery store and grocery store clerking was all he had ever known, and he needed to do something to support himself while, in his free time, he practiced his craft, the craft that he hoped would one day become his livelihood: stand-up comedy. He had never done stand-up comedy before. He wasn't particularly funny either; in fact, he was a very serious, boring person. But all his life he had wanted to be up there on stage making faces and farting noises and dirty jokes and ultimately making people laugh, so he would have to practice hard. And he couldn't continue to get drunk every night, as he had done throughout his entire college career. Getting drunk with that kind of frequency wasn't in his cards anymore. He had to work in the daytime and so the nighttime was the only time he had to develop his comedic skills. There was no use or excuse for coming home from work, collapsing onto the couch, turning on the tv and drinking himself into a silly pile of flesh.

"That's what grocery store clerks do," he always told himself, paying no attention to what he was.

Hogan Marsupial was proud of his newfound idealistic attitude. Unfortunately, like most newfound idealistic attitudes, this one was short-lived: for two weeks he worked at the grocery store from eight to six, and for two weeks he came home from work, exhausted, and collapsed onto the couch, turned on the tv and drank himself into a silly pile of flesh. Every morning he would wake up with a screaming hangover that he would scream back at and then he would scream at himself, first of all for being such a lush, second of all for not practicing his craft, not even doing one funny thing the night before. It really depressed him. Even making a few obscene phone calls or walking to the toilet and back (which he did every ten minutes or so) like Charlie Chaplin would have passed, in his eyes, as movements towards becoming a more proficient stand-up comedian. Even looking in the mirror and sticking his tongue out at himself—it would have been something. But he did nothing. He sat there on his couch and watched sitcom after sitcom in drunken, blank-faced inertia.

Then one night, the first night of his third full week in Hollywood, Marsupial snapped. On the way home from work he didn't stop by the liquor store to purchase the usual case of Rolling Rock. Instead, he purchased a jelly-filled donut and a cup of stale, greasy coffee. The coffee gave him a furious case of diarrhea but after two hours on the toilet the diarrhea was gone, and he spent the rest of the evening practicing his craft. He practiced without a break and without a drink until the sun came up and the next morning he went into the grocery store and handed in his resignation. (Later that afternoon he realized he might have made a mistake. The grocery store had been a steady source of income and he had no idea what stand-up comedy paid, especially when you were just starting out. But if worse came to worse he decided he would call up his parents and leech off of them. It wouldn't be the first time . . .)

Getting a gig wasn't as easy as Marsupial thought it would be, despite all of his hard work the night before. The first place he went was a ritzy hotel—a Ritz Carlton, actually—and there was a line full of stand-up comics snaking out the entranceway and around the block.

"What's everybody waiting for?" Marsupial asked the last person in line, a bony, scruffy man with vegetable stains all over his body. The man gave Marsupial a once over. He toked on his cigarette and said, "Interview."

"Interview?" Marsupial replied. "You mean, we have to be *interviewed?*"

But the man ignored him now. He took a final drag of his cigarette and flicked it into the gutter, then lit a fresh one. Marsupial asked him if he could bum a cigarette. The man asked him, "Can I put my cigarette out on your fuckin face?"

"Oh," said Marsupial . . . and after a short pause ran away. Not because he was afraid of getting his face burnt and dirty—he had asked more than a few people if he could bum cigarettes in the past and received far cruder responses— but because he was afraid of the interview. Stand-up comics had to undergo interviews? He hated interviews, hated them. Even the interview for the grocery store, a short laid-back dialogue with the store's short laid-back manager, had been grueling for him. One of the reasons he always wanted to be a stand-up comic was because he thought all you had to do to get a gig was walk into a hotel or club or bar and start telling jokes and doing impressions of Jack Nicholson. If people laughed at you, eventually the right person would approach you and put you on stage; if people didn't laugh at you, eventually you'd get the picture and go somewhere else. Where and when this assumption had come into Marsupial's possession escaped him, but there it was, and now, having spoken to one of his rude but informative colleagues, there it went.

Hogan Marsupial drank a gallon of red wine that night, cabernet sauvignon, the thickest and the driest, and the meanest in terms of the brutality of the hangovers it produced, but that's what Marsupial wanted, a brutal hangover, because once that brutality wore off he would feel that much more refreshed, as he felt after every hangover slipped away, usually at some point in the late afternoon, but this one was going to last two days, he wasn't going to counteract the wine with excesses of water or aspirin or pizza or anything, and afterwards, after the head-pounding and the nausea and the shakes and the coldsweats ceased to exist, he would climb out of the flames and, with a mighty squawk, flap his ambitious wings.

After Marsupial climbed out of the flames and squawked, he called his parents and asked them to wire him some money. Then he ate some breakfast, threw it up in the kitchen sink, drank a cup of his favorite blend of bitter instant coffee, and hit the streets, determined to find a stage that would accompany him without first dragging him over the coals of an interview. By noon he had found nothing, so he went home and threw up again, then took a nap. He got up at sundown and decided to stay in for the evening . . . but just as his ass was about to make contact with his couch, he was struck by an unexpected, unsupressible bolt of ambition.

He hit the streets again. By 9:00, he had found what he was looking for.

The name of the place was Dagwood's. It was possibly the scummiest hole-in-the-wall he had ever set foot in. Scum on the floors, scum on the walls, scum on the ceiling, scum on the furniture, scum in the beer—scum everywhere—and strong-smelling scum at that. The stage consisted of a little cobweb-ridden foot stool that had been thrown in a dark corner. Marsupial wouldn't even have noticed it unless the bar tender and owner of Dagwood's, who raised a lip corner when Marsupial laid his Jack Nicholson impression on him, pointed it out.

"Knock yourself out," shrugged the bar tender, and disappeared behind the bar counter.

Ankle-high in scum, Marsupial waded his way over to the "stage". Halfway there he got nervous and waded back to the bar, waited for the bartender to reappear and serve him one, two, three shots of Tequila, which he slammed without salt or lime. Now he was ready. Now he was confident in himself and his power to induce hilarity. Now he strode over to the foot stool and leapt up onto it and faced his audience, and began his routine.

Marsupial's audience consisted of two bearded hobos, one fairly chubby, one a virtual skeleton, both drunk out of their skulls and shifting back and forth between lip-smacking consciousness into log-sawing unconsciousness. But Marsupial had no idea they were drunk. He had no idea anybody was anything. He should have. He had a less than canny ability to read and relate to people, but he should have at least been able to recognize that these two hobos had tippled themselves into stark idiocy. Then again, he was a little tipsy himself now. But more than that, much more than that . . . he was on stage. On stage! And that's what it was:

Stagefright.

Since he had never been on stage before, he had never experienced stagefright, except when he found himself in front of a urinal in a crowded public restroom, unable to urinate even though his bladder was filled to the rim, but that was a different kind of stagefright than the kind that was oppressing him now. It was perhaps the ugliest, nastiest, darkest feeling that had ever plagued his mind and body. It was as if he had been thrown into a tank full of liquid poison ivy that seeped into his open pores and surged through his bloodstream and like a wave crashed all over his brain and now that brain was cranking out impossibly itchy thoughts. He wanted to crack open his skull and scratch his brain to smithereens. He couldn't think. He couldn't move. And yet he was moving and thinking . . . and talking. What was he saying? He didn't know, he didn't know. What *did* he know? The earth is round, the universe is expanding, yesterday my girlfriend said I had no manners and I said to her I says monkey see monkey do-do . . . Wait, did I just say that? Was that part of my routine? What is my routine? Do I even have a routine? What the hell am I doing up here? Are words coming out of my mouth? What are words? Am I blowing it? Am I a total jackass? Am I even *alive* . . . ?

Even though his mind felt like a rotten tossed salad, Hogan Marsupial managed to bumble through ten minutes of his routine before things got ugly. His routine was . . . not funny. Every now and then one of the hobos would giggle—once there was the sound of a cackle—but the impetus for the giggling and the cackle wasn't Marsupial's language and mannerisms, it was the infantile dreams they were having when they were unconscious. The bar tender didn't laugh, since he wasn't there (he had slipped out to a bar across the street for a glass of decent scotch), and the waitress didn't laugh either, since she wasn't listening (she was too busy chewing on her fingernails and applying and re-applying makeup, bright pastel makeup all over her craggy face). But even if everybody there had been laughing at Marsupial, and even if everybody there had amounted to three thousand as opposed to three people, he wouldn't have been aware of it. Too stagefrightened. Still, he was able to put words together in something like an orderly manner, insofar as orderly means the signification of his words could more or less be understood by other English-speaking people. The words weren't funny. Most of the words were as colorless, flat and dull as Marsupial the man. But at least he was able to produce them. At least he wasn't speaking in tongues, although speaking in tongues would have probably been a lot funnier. And yet, whether he was funny or boring or intelligible or gibbering like a chimp—nothing could have prohibited the death of the audience.

Hairy people sweat more than smooth-skinned people. The rule isn't an absolute—there are plenty of people with baby's bottoms for hides that sweat like hogs at the trough—but it holds true more often than not. Hogan Marsupial was a fairly hairy person. He didn't have any hair on his back, but he had a lot of hair on his chest and stomach and legs. The hair was long. Curly, and long. Some of the hairs on his chest, if he grabbed hold of them with his fingertips and stretched them out, measured over three inches; and when he wore t-shirts he always looked heavier than he actually was, the hair on his gut adding a little something to his girth, which was already beleaguered by a modest but not invisible beer belly. At any rate, Marsupial sweat like a bunch of glued together shower heads, sometimes without even physically exerting himself. Sometimes sitting on his couch and staring too hard at the tv was enough to get his glands flowing; but since he never exercised, never even walked down the street too fast if he could help it, usually his nerves, his bear trap nerves, ready to snap at the slightest nibble, were the instigators, and that he was both a naturally hairy and a naturally anxious person was an annoying misfortune. The sweating always started in his eyebrows and armpits—these were the hairiest places on his body, not because the hair there was longer and curlier than on his torso and legs but because there the pores out of which his hair follicles grew were much closer together—then spread down his face and down his body, and kept on spreading until either his nerves settled, or he took an ice cold shower, or, in extreme cases, he took a Xanax or a

Vicodin. But he tried to stay away from drugs of this sort since every time he swallowed one he became an uncontrollable addict.

In an 1839 notebook entry, the Danish philosopher Søren Kierkegaard writes, "All existence makes me anxious, from the smallest fly to the mysteries of the Incarnation; the whole thing is inexplicable to me, I myself most of all; to me all existence is infected, I myself most of all. Thus I crouch here and tremble." Anybody familiar with Kierkegaard will know that these words are definitively Kierkegaardian. At the same time, anybody familiar with Marsupial will know that they are definitively Marsupialian. (As for whether or not Kierkegaard had a thick carpet of hair growing all over his body and sweat a lot, well, he never wrote about it in his notebook.)

Since he was old enough to know he was alive, Marsupial could remember being nervous, often for no reason at all. It was especially traumatizing during his prepubescent years. One moment he would be playing with his toys or watching cartoons, the next he would be wide-eyed and quivering, wondering why he was wide-eyed and quivering and powerless to do anything about it. Things got worse when he actually had a reason to be nervous: he would pass out, or vomit, or piss and shit in his pants, or demolish everyone and everything he could get his hands on—namely himself. He had only demolished himself three or four times, always during the most nerve-wracked periods of his life; the worst beating his body had ever received from his fists and teeth occurred after he locked his sister in a garbage can and a garbage man accidentally poured her into a garbage truck and ground her up. But even the feeling that that act of violence invoked in him didn't compare to the feeling that was being invoked right now, at Dagwood's, in front of two drunk hobos and one Technicolor-faced waitress, by the stage beneath his feet. It was a feeling so wracked with nerve that consciously assaulting himself or anybody else in any way was not even an option. Nor could he pass out, or vomit, or piss or shit—these psychosomatic products of his dread were too weak to express the dread. His body needed something more robust, more biting. Something that could represent the stagefrightened state of his mind in all of its shining nastiness.

For ten minutes Marsupial's body, as it stood there gesticulating and sweating in front of the crowd, couldn't conceive of an adequate means of expression. Then, suddenly, his body got an idea . . . and his sweat glands, rather than continuing to produce and emit sweat, began to produce and emit a poisonous gas that, the moment it washed over the inattentive hobos and waitress, not only crystallized their lungs and heart on the spot, it vaporized their skin and flesh, and their skeletons and internal organs fell to the ground with a lardy, sopping plop. If his body could have smiled on its own, it would have. This lethal, carnage-inducing toxin that Marsupial's sweat glands were now disseminating throughout the bar was the perfect representation of the anxiety that his mind was now disseminating throughout his body. Of course, Marsupial himself was immune to the toxin. He was also completely unaware of it, as well as its effects. Stagefrightened to an inexplicably monstrous degree, he didn't notice that the audience had turned into little pools of gore, let alone that his sweat glands were responsible for it. He was having a difficult enough time trying to articulate his routine to concentrate on what was going on all around him—and, for that matter, on what was going on inside him. And when his routine finally came to an end, he still didn't notice anything: like an ashamed and embarrassed child, Marsupial, head bent, literally sprinted out of Dagwood's, convinced the routine had stunk, convinced he was a moron and a waste of space, wanting to get the hell out of there before the audience had a chance to boo and spit on and throw sandwiches at him.

The instant Marsupial stepped off stage, his sweat glands stopped producing poison and started producing sweat again.

II

Marsupial spent the next week in a drunken haze. Occasionally the haze cleared and revealed a stripper dancing on his lap, but for the most part his reality was a black hole, and when he finally ran out of money and had no choice but to sober up, he recalled nothing of the week before except for all the lap dancing strippers and a few handfuls of dreams. Most of the dreams were boring and uneventful; others were nightmares involving plane crashes and chase sequences, among other things. In one of the nightmares Marsupial bumped into a movie star who had a shrunken head growing out of his elbow. It was kind of cute. It looked like a little bonsai tree with its wild, kinked hair. Marsupial, trying to be friendly, said, "Neat head," but the movie star thought he was making fun of him so he tore the shrunken head off of his elbow and hurled the bloody thing at Marsupial's face. The head had tiny arms and hands on its cheeks and when it hit his face it grabbed onto his lips and swung itself over to his shoulder. Perched there like a bird, it smiled at him and said, "That'll be fifty dollars, sweetie." Then it shrieked like a lobster under the knife.

III

Penniless and hung over, Hogan Marsupial called his parents and asked them for more money. They asked him what happened to the money they had given him the week before. He said, "Hollywood's expensive, you guys." His parents waited for him to expand on and ornament this excuse for an excuse but he didn't: that's all he gave them. To say the least, Mr. and Mrs. Marsupial were less than thrilled with their son, as a person and as an excuse maker. "But then again there's something to be said for the appalling simplicity of Hogan's excuse," Mr. Marsupial remarked later that evening to his wife as they lay in bed blinking at the ceiling. "I mean, he could have bullshitted us till the cows came home and sat in it but he only gave us a little whiff of bullshit. Not even a whiff. What Hogan said in so few words was so much bullshit it's not even bullshit, it's a hearty affirmation of his total unwillingness to oppress us, his loving parents, with bullshit. Which is bullshit in itself, but still, I can appreciate and even admire that kind of bullshit. That's my boy. I'll wire him a few thousand dollars in the morning."

When Marsupial received the wire transfer, he headed straight for the liquor store, but on the way there he had an epiphany, just like Stephen Daedelus near the end of *Portrait of the Artist as a Young Man*, he told himself, remembering the only book he had read in college from start to finish (even though he majored in English), only Marsupial's epiphany, unlike Daedelus's, didn't occur on a beach and there were no seductive mermaids involved. In a flashbulb of perspicacity, Marsupial, gawking into the front window of the liquor store, suddenly realized that binge drinking with the zeal and fortitude of a thirsty bulldog was not only unhealthy, it wasn't conducive to the development of his craft—which, unbeknownst to himself until that epiphanic moment, he had not given up after all.

On the way to the liquor store after his performance last week, Marsupial had concluded that he was no stand-up comedian and never would be, no matter how hard he practiced; he had no business, no business at all, making scatological wise-cracks on a stage; his business was being a polite, anonymous grocery store clerk. But now he felt differently. Now, immersed in the bright blue waters of epiphany, Marsupial felt that he couldn't tolerate his existence unless he existed not as a polite, anonymous grocery store clerk but as a lewd, belittling, foul-mouthed, renowned stand-up comedian. And if Hogan Marsupial was ever going to exist in that capacity he had to stop carrying on like the hobos he unknowingly killed the other night at Dagwood's. He had to get control of himself, to overcome himself. He had to get back on the horse that had kicked him off. No more booze, no more blackouts, no more feeling sorry for himself. The world was his oyster and he would take hold of the world and pry it open and suck out its blubber and gargle with it. Then he would spit the blubber out into the faces of the audience, and bathe in their laughter and applause

. . .

Marsupial's epiphany lasted two minutes. After it passed, he decided to get drunk one more time before beginning his new positively charged life. He drank for three days and nights, then took a nap and a cold shower, threw up, swallowed four capsules of aspirin, drank two cans of soda pop, a liter of orange juice, a two-liter of Spring Water and a pot of coffee, ate breakfast, threw up again, and went back to Dagwood's, feeling lightheaded but also feeling enthusiastic, and confident, and strong.

"Been lookin for you," said the bar tender as Marsupial brushed a membrane of scum off of a bar stool and sat on it. "Where you been for the last week?"

Marsupial's face crinkled up. "I don't know?" He was telling the truth. But even if he had known where he had been he would have responded the same way. Why did the bar tender care about his whereabouts? He had come back here to beg for a second chance on stage and the last thing he expected was the bar tender to ask him anything other than if he would please go away and never come back. But here he was taking a genuine interest in him. Marsupial was immediately suspicious. He uncrinkled his face and said, "Why?"

The bar tender finished the cigarette he was smoking and chased it with a shot of Southern Comfort. He chased the Southern Comfort with a shot of Hot Damn. Then he wiped his lips off on his forearm and said, "Well, y'know how you were like doin a routine or somethin last week? I mean, y'know how you were like standin up there in front of everybody and tellin jokes and shit? Whaddya call that shit you do? Makin people laugh, like. There's a name for that shit isn't there? Whaddya call that shit?"

"Uhm," said Marsupial.

The bar tender lit another cigarette. "Whatever. Anyway, I don't know if you noticed or not but I hadda run across the street and I only saw the first minute or two of your thing there. Actually that's not true. Truth is, I didn't see any of it. I wasn't payin attention. I was actually pretty drunk and stoned and I'll tell you something when I'm drunk and stoned I don't pay attention to much of anything. But that's not true either. Truth is, I pay attention to some things when I'm drunk and stoned. I just pay attention to more things when I'm not. But the thing is, the thing I wanna tell you . . . what was it? Oh yeah. When I came back here, when I came back here even more drunk and stoned than I was before I left, d'you know what I found? Do you? Guess."

"Uhm," said Marsupial.

"I'll tell you what I found. I'll tell you right now. I found—a bunch of dead people!"

Marsupial frowned. "A bunch of dead people?"

"That's right. A bunch of dead people."

"What's that supposed to mean? What's that supposed to mean?"

"I don't know. You tell me."

Not a peep from Marsupial now. Trying to figure out the meaning of what had been said to him, he sat there frozen on the bar stool like a popsicle on a stick. He didn't even make an attempt to wipe off the spittle that the bar tender's mouth had sprayed all over his face.

The bar tender left him hanging there for a few seconds. Then he threw back his head and burst into laugher. The laughter, while it was clearly laughter, sounded more like a cow hollering as cars ran over it one after another, and all of Dagwood's customers—tonight they consisted of four sloshed, kaleidoscopically dressed pimps—looked over at him and kinked their lips. Their lips kinked more and more as the bar tender's laughter magnified and soon the lips had reached their limit. They couldn't be kinked a hair's breadth more and the pimps had no choice but to ignore the laughter and mind their own business, which was impossible to do as long as the laughter persisted. So the pimps simulated ignoring the laughter and minding their own business. Lucky for them it was not long afterwards that the laughter came to a screeching halt and the bar tender, pardoning himself, as if he had just farted but wasn't very sorry about it, told him what had happened . . .

After the bar tender returned from across the street, he climbed up onto the bar counter and took a power nap. During the nap he didn't have any dreams. This was not unusual. "I was born without a unconscious," he said, "and I've never had a dream in my whole shit-stained life." When he woke he made a pot of coffee and it wasn't until he was halfway through his second cup that he realized something wasn't right. So he said to the waitress and the hobos, "Everything all right?" Nobody answered him. He baby-stepped over to the corpse piles and poked at them with a fork. By reflex, one of the hobo's eyes, "which was like this big peanut lodged in this big mound of shit," blinked. The bar tender yelped and passed out. Again he dreamt no dreams. While he was passed out he soiled himself, and when he woke he was being stared at by a face that was looming over him and pinching it's nose. "Hiya," said the bar tender. "You smell," said the face. The face added, "What the hell's going on here?" The bar tender was clueless. He scrambled into the back room and cleaned himself up, then called the police. The police said they were busy, call back in a while. He did. A squad car arrived fifteen minutes later and a donut-logged man in a police uniform with a handlebar mustache squeezed out of it and into Dagwood's.

"What's the problem," said the cop.

"Dead people," said the bar tender.

The cop nodded. He got down on his knees—he had so many donuts crammed inside his body this took another fifteen minutes—and examined one of the corpse piles with short, sharp sniffs. "Yep. Dead all right." The bar tender asked what needed to be done. "First thing," the cop said, looking up at him, "is to figure out why these people are dead. Any ideas?"

The bar tender told him what he knew about Marsupial. He told him how Marsupial asked him if he could stand up in front of everybody and tell jokes, and how the bar tender said, "Knock yourself out," and how he didn't pay attention to Marsupial knocking himself out, and how he went across the street to drink a real drink, and how he came back and took a nap and woke up and drank some coffee and Marsupial was gone, and everybody was dead, and . . . "That's all I know," the bar tender confessed. The cop, still on his knees, waited to respond to him until he was on his feet again. Fifteen minutes later he panted, "You say this guy was telling jokes?"

"That's right. He was a joke teller."

The cop grabbed onto one of his mustache's handlebars and revved it like a motorcycle, something he often did when he was processing information. "Funny?"

"Dunno."

"Dunno?"

"I told you I wasn't listenin to him."

"Why not?"

"Because."

"I see."

The cop let go of his mustache, took out a notepad and scribbled something down in it. He tried to hide what he was scribbling from the bar tender and the bar tender tried not to look like he was sneaking a peek at what he was scribbling out of the corners of his eyes. Both failed: the bar tender saw what the cop was scribbling—an addition to his grocery list: two dozen porridge-filled donuts with multicolored sprinkles—and the cop saw that the bar tender was peeking at what he was scribbling. Then the cop asked if he could use the toilet. The bar tender pointed it out. An hour passed before the cop returned. The bar tender was on the phone. He was being won over by a credit card salesman and was just about to order his twenty-second VISA when the cop cleared his throat. Startled, the bar tender dropped the phone onto the floor. It shattered like a wine glass . . . because it was a wine glass. The cop sneezed and said, "Here's the way I see it. This perp Marsupial—he ain't no murderer. He's a killer all right—the reason these people are in this kinda shape is because of that funny bastard—but he had no intent to kill. What he had was an intent to amuse. He came in here tonight with the premeditation of making people laugh. Obviously he's done that. Obviously, he's made these people laugh so hard they've not only keeled over dead, they've . . . well, they've melted. They laughed and laughed and laughed and they couldn't stop laughing and they got so hot they just up and liquefied like ice cubes in an oven. You say you didn't hear his routine but nobody needs to hear it to know what happened here. The evidence speaks for itself. This bastard Marsupial is funny as hell and these victims are victims because they've listened to him and laughed themselves to death. He didn't murder them, he killed them. But there's no law against killing. Case closed." This said, the cop ordered a pitcher of beer, chugged it, used the toilet again and left. Before going he told the bar tender he had to promise to mop up and dispose of the corpse piles in the next twenty-four hours. If he didn't promise, the cop would either have to fine him $1,000 or take away his liquor license for an indefinite amount of time.

. . . The bar tender paused. He told Marsupial not to go anywhere and went to serve the pimps another round of beers. Marsupial no longer sat on the bar stool like a popsicle on a stick; he sat there like a fistful of mud on a stick. Had he really been responsible for the deadly meltdowns of these three people? More importantly—*had he really been funny?*

When the bar tender returned he asked Marsupial if he wanted to take a walk. "Don't you want me to go on tonight?" whined Marsupial. The bar tender grinned. He said, "Yeah, sure. But not right now. Let's go on a walk right now. I got some shit to tell you." Marsupial was reticent to go. He worried that his audience would decrease or disappear altogether by the time he got back, but had it not been for this bar tender he wouldn't have a gig in the first place. So he bowed his head, peeled his body off of the bar stool and walked out into the neon streets of Hollywood.

"Keep an eye on the place for me, will you fellas?" said the bar tender as he followed Marsupial out the door. Two of the pimps nodded, one shrugged. The other one nodded, then shrugged, then nodded again, unsure of which physical response was more appropriate. In the end he decided it would be better to respond verbally since physical responses had more of a tendency to be misinterpreted. But he couldn't think of anything to say, and by then the bar tender was gone.

As the two men walked down Baldwin Boulevard, threading through heaps of garbage and gaggles of loitering rappers and movie stars, the bar tender chattered Marsupial's ear off. Most of what he said concerned his own life and troubles. Marsupial listened to him patiently, wondering where it was all going. Then the bar tender said, "You're probably wondering where I'm going with all this, right? Shit, I don't know. I'm just trying to get you to like me, I guess. Do you like me? I worry too much about whether or not people like me and shit. That's a bad thing. You can't go though life worrying about every single little thing people may or may not be thinking about you. But I do. Well, I do when I'm sober. And I'm only sober for about thirty seconds every morning. So I guess I don't care what you think about me. Go ahead and think I'm a piece of shit, I don't care. Fact is, I am a piece of shit. But none of this shit has anything to do with why I asked you to take a walk with me."

Marsupial and the bar tender passed a garbage heap in which Tom Cruise, one of Marsupial's favorite actors, was standing and talking to three lesser-known but still famous actors. He wanted to go over and shake Tom's hand and tell him how much he liked him but he knew he could get arrested for it. Some cops would arrest him for even looking at Tom Cruise, although in a court of law it would have to be proven that the intent of the look was to approach and praise, and that was difficult to do without photographs and video recordings of the look. Still, Marsupial decided to play it safe and position his eyes elsewhere.

"Look, where are we going?" said Marsupial. "Can't we just go back to Dagwood's please? Can't you just let me do my routine please? I'm getting really antsy."

"Not too antsy, I hope," the bar tender replied, then grabbed Marsupial by the elbow and swung him into a dark, dripping alley. The bar tender maintained his grip on Marsupial's elbow and ushered him to the far end of the alley. As they went he explained everything to him. Maruspial only picked up bits and pieces of the explanation—the bar tender was very excited; words were sprinting out of his mouth like flames from a flamethrower—but the bits and pieces were enough for him to figure out what was going on.

As far as Marsupial could tell, after the cop had left Dagwood's last week, the bar tender called another bar tender. This second bar tender bar tended at and owned The Brown Tooth, an upscale bar (compared to Dagwood's) on Streep Street that featured some kind of live entertainment every night (anything from music to poetry readings to circus freak exhibitions), and those who performed made decent money, anywhere from $150 to $500 a night. Dagwood's bar tender told The Brown Tooth's bar tender all about this joke teller Marsupial who was so funny people literally died laughing at him. "Bring him over here *right now*," said The Brown Tooth's bar tender. Dagwood's bar tender told him he'd like to but he had no idea where Marsupial ran off to, or where he lived, or anything. It occurred to him that he didn't even know Marsupial's name. The Brown Tooth's bar tender told him that if and when he ran into Marsupial again to bring him right over and he would put him on. Dagwood's bar tender agreed under the condition that he was paid twenty percent of Marsupial's earnings. "You can have a hundred percent of it for all I care," said The Brown Tooth's bar tender, "but that's between you and the talent." Dagwood's bar tender responded to this response with a contemplative frog face—he demonstrated the face for Marsupial—and as he guided Marsupial a little further down the alley and then pushed him through a small black door and into a kitchen full of short overworked Aryans in dishwashing uniforms, he said it was only fair that his "finder's fee" be not twenty but one hundred percent of Marsupial's paycheck and it would be "cruddy" not to mention "totally shitty" of Marsupial to complain about it. After all, he was about to get some serious exposure here. By the end of the night he may even have a contract with a Big Name agency. "This is your break," said the bar tender. "You've been discovered and shit. You're practically a millionaire. You're practically famous as hell. Long as you don't screw it up tonight, you're the man. Can you dig that shit?"

The bar tender shut up. At last. Marsupial had a million things to say to him but couldn't manage to get one thing out, and before he knew it he was flung through two swinging saloon doors into The Brown Tooth proper.

It was big. And green, very green. The walls were green and the floor and ceiling and lights and tables were green and even some of the people sitting and drinking and smoking at the tables were wearing green outfits. The stage was green, too. It was as if Marsupial had walked smack into the middle of a lime. He stood there dumbly, trying to adjust his eyes to the scene, trying to figure out why this place wasn't called The Green Tooth. Meanwhile Dagwood's bar tender hurried over to the bar and consulted with The Brown Tooth's bar tender, who then hurried over to Marsupial and introduced himself. He told him he had heard a lot about him and was happy to have him aboard and the next act wasn't for a half hour would he like to go on right now? Marsupial was still unable to respond. The bar tenders took his inability as a yes and led him up and onto the stage. Dagwood's bar tender whispered encouragement in Marsupial's ear as The Brown Tooth's bar tender grabbed a microphone and introduced him to the audience. "All right folks," he said, "we've got a special treat for you tonight. I hope you've all been to church and made your peace with God this week because right now you're going to leave this carny outhouse of an existence we call life in a convulsion of lung-throttling glee. Yes indeed. Put your hands together, ladies and genitals, for. . ."

The bar tender frowned. He covered the mic with his hand and, keeping his head still, reached towards Marsupial with his lips. "Psst. What's your name?"

Marsupial thought about the question for a moment but couldn't come up with an answer. "I can't come up with an answer," he admitted. The Brown Tooth's bar tender's face scrunched up and he shook it at him in disbelief. This gesture caused Marsupial first to scrunch up his face and shake it back at him, then to remember his name. With the enthusiasm of a child who has found an Easter egg he spouted, "Hogan! Hogan Marsupial!"

The Brown Tooth's bar tender nodded and removed his hand from the mic. "Give it up for Mr. Hogan . . . 'The Hogan' Marsupial! All right!" He often made up little on-the-spot nicknames for performers and was particularly proud of this one, in spite of its brazen lack of creativity. But for some unknown reason he found the name Hogan hilarious.

Wooden, disinterested applause from the audience ensued as the two bar tenders scurried off stage. The audience consisted of about twenty people, not a big crowd, but a lot bigger than what Marsupial had been faced with at Dagwood's last week. It absolutely terrified him. So did the stage beneath his feet and the microphone in front of his face, both of which were very real. He wasn't standing on some moldy foot stool in a dark corner anymore. This was The Big Show.

Then he got to thinking about how his routine had been lethally funny.

It was almost impossible for him to believe. How could he think he was so awful and everybody else think he was so funny? It didn't make any sense. On the other hand, Dagwood's bar tender had no reason to lie to him. He was obviously friends with The Brown Tooth's bar tender and wouldn't bring him some damn schlep that would make both bar tenders look bad, whether he was the one getting paid or not.

But Marsupial didn't want to kill anybody. He wanted to make people laugh, but he didn't want them to die from it, and he certainly didn't want them to melt . . . or did he? No, no, he didn't. Ideally he would like people to laugh at him and live. But if he was too funny to achieve that ideal, what could he do? He would rather have people laugh at him and die than not laugh at him and live. He couldn't deny it. If he had to choose between being a killer and a bore, he would kill. But could he muster up the comedic energy it would take to kill this audience tonight? And not just a few members of the audience, but all of them. Ten or even fifteen of them wouldn't be enough: he had to demolish them all, including both bar tenders; he would feel altogether inadequate if he didn't. But if he destroyed the bar tenders who would get him his next gig? Not to mention that one or more of the audience members might be a talent scout. No chance of his name getting around town by word of mouth if all the mouths were dead. Well, he would have to take it easy on everybody tonight. He would have to omit the funnier portions of his routine and settle for just making people giggle hard instead of cackling themselves into slimy remnants. Later, when he was a full-fledged celebrity and had more clout— then he could do as he pleased. For now he would have to suck it up.

Marsupial spent fifteen seconds coming to this conclusion. During that time he simply stood in the middle of the stage, shoulders slumped, arms dangling, head bent, staring down at the green, green floorboards beneath his feet. Between the tenth and fifteenth second the audience started to get restless; some even began fishing through their pockets and purses for food to throw at him. But then Marsupial took a deep breath, straightened up and began his routine.

And stagefright immediately landed on him like a monster truck coming off a jump.

And Marsupial had no idea what he was saying, or who he was, or why he had been born.

And Marsupial's mind told his body to tell his sweat glands to compensate for the terror by transmuting the sweat they were spitting out of his pores into poison and spitting that out with twice the intensity, twice the fury.

A few minutes later the audience and the bar tenders, and even the little spiders that lived in the corners of the ceiling, all resembled burnt goulash.

Again, Marsupial had no idea. He knew his lips were in motion, he knew there were sounds coming out of his mouth, and he knew he was standing on his feet; otherwise the world was just a big green blur. He wondered if the world would stay that way. Could he live inside of a big green blur for the rest of his life? But maybe the world had always been this way, maybe he had been born into the blur. Which was not an appealing thought. Which made him want to go get drunk again. But if he was living in a blur how could he see through it to the bottle of booze that needed to be picked up and poured inside of him? Could bottles of booze even exist inside of a blur? Isn't the only thing that can exist inside of a blur . . . a bunch of blurs?

He didn't know. But he managed to get drunk before and he would manage to get drunk again, regardless of his recent epiphany and commitment to remain sober and ambitious. This time he didn't even make it to the end of his routine—not that it mattered—before he scrambled off the stage and darted out of The Brown Tooth, totally oblivious to what looked like a room full of people that had had a dump truck full of hot lava poured all over them. If anybody had been alive to see him go they would have laughed, or at least smirked, since as he ran he kept socking himself in the gut and slapping himself in the face—punishment for stinking so badly and for being such a boring loser. He kept running and socking and slapping himself until he came to a strip bar. There he stopped running and stopped socking himself in the gut, although he did continue to whale on his face for a while. But eventually he stopped that, too.

Half an hour later he was drunk and whispering fragments of Romantic poetry, most of which belonged to John Keats, into the ear of a stripper. He continued to drink and whisper poetry into strippers' ears until he ran out of money again, two weeks later, and had to call his parents and ask them for more.

"What happened to the three thousand we sent you?" said his father.

"I was mugged by a movie star," said Marsupial. "No, a rapper, I mean. I mean—"

His parents hung up on him. He called them back a few minutes later and the answering machine answered. It said, "Hello. This is the Marsupial residence. Mr. and Mrs. Marsupial live here and we have a son named Hogan. He's a bum and a leech and a drunk, but we love him. We're not giving him any more money, though. Leave a message. Goodbye."

Marsupial, sober now, spent a few seconds deliberating his options. The way he saw it, he had two. He could stay here in Hollywood and get his old job at the grocery store back, or he could move back home, back to Ohio, "the heart of it all" according to all of the welcome signs on the highway. It would have been nice if he had enough money to get drunk; that way, he could take his time thinking about which option to choose. But he only had enough money to get a buzz. And a dull buzz at that.

So Marsupial decided to go home. He hitchhiked and used the few cents in his pocket to buy some moldy beef jerky.

"Hello," he said to his parents when he got home. They said hello back and asked him how he was doing. "Fair," he said . . . and threw up all over the walls. Then he fainted.

When he woke up, he was in rehab.

He was laying on a white bed that was surrounded by white walls and a white ceiling and floor, and everybody walking around was wearing white suits of armor and face masks.

Marsupial was nude. There were no covers on his bed.

"Can I have some clothes?" he rasped.

"No," whispered a female voice. "But would you like me to do a strip tease for you?"

Marsupial nodded his head as fast as he could nod it. The owner of the female voice leapt up on his bed and ripped off all of her armor, but she kept the face mask on. Marsupial hooted. The owner of the female voice gyrated her hips, squeezed her breasts together, slapped her ass, blew him a loud kiss. Marsupial wanted to blow her a kiss back, but he found that he lacked the energy to pucker up his lips. Offended, the owner of the female voice stopped dancing, climbed off his bed and put her armor back on. She gave him an injection of something and three blinks later he was out cold.

When he woke up, he was living in the basement of his parent's house.

He had never envisioned himself living with his parents after college and had always scoffed at people who did that. Now he scoffed at himself. But all things considered, it really wasn't too bad, living there. He had his own room and his own tv and vcr and he and his parents got along all right, and his mother did all of his laundry and cooked for him, too. It wasn't long before Marsupial was back in rehab, though, trying in vain to pucker up his lips, and for the next ten years he proceeded to move back and forth between the rehab facility and his parent's basement, working for the grocery store his father owned when he was clean and sober. He never went on stage again, and so he never got stagefright and killed anybody again. Nor did he tell a dirty joke, or impersonate a movie star, or exaggerate a belch or a fart, or simulate masturbation, or simulate having sex with a porcupine, or pretend he was a drag queen, or make exotic bird calls, or do anything else that funny people do—nothing he did was even remotely amusing. During those ten years he was more serious and boring than he had ever been prior to moving out to Hollywood, and it wasn't until his liver fell apart and he was laying on his death bed that the desire to become a stand-up comedian returned to him. But by then it was too late. All he could do was grunt for a nurse and, when she came to him, all he could do was make these half-hearted animal noises.

Amused, the nurse snickered.

Then she flipped Marsupial over onto his stomach and stuck a thermometer in his rear.

A CONCERN

"Can I seriously wonder whether my body is made of glass, or whether I am naked in my bed? If I can, then I am obliged to doubt even my own body. On the other hand, my body is saved if my meditation remains quite distinct from madness and dreams."

—Michel Foucault, "My Body, This Paper, This Fire"

He woke up looking down on his body. Apparently he had disembodied in his sleep and floated up, up, up, rotating 180 degrees in the process, like a shish kebab over flames, because now he was laying on the ceiling. His back was chilly, so chilly. His body, made visible by a bright beam of moonlight shooting through the bedroom window, lay on the bed, outside the covers (he always sleeps outside the covers), on its back (he always sleeps on his back), in the nude (on Sunday nights he sleeps in a fig leaf). Its eyes were wide open. He always sleeps with his eyes wide open so he couldn't tell if the body was sleeping or looking back at him. He decided to ask it.

"Are you looking at me?" he whispered.

No response. The ceiling was a long way from the bed, so maybe the body couldn't hear him. But if it was looking at him it should have been able to see his lips move. Do his lips move when he speaks? When he's in his body they do. But he's never been out of his body before so he doesn't know whether or not his out-of-body lips move when he speaks. Maybe he should pinch them and say something, to see if they move. But if he pinches his lips he won't be able to open them and say anything. Can he even pinch his lips? Do his lips even exist anymore? Do the fingers that want to pinch them so badly exist? His body exists: he can see it if he arches his head up a little and peers down at it. And it's not see-through either. Usually disembodied bodies are see-through. So he's heard. Anyway his body isn't see-through and he bets his lips aren't see-through either. He would like to kiss his body's lips with his out-of-body lips. Maybe that will wake his body up, a kiss . . . if, that is, his body is sleeping, and not dead.

He once died in a fast food restaurant. One second he was standing there ordering a cheeseburger, fries and soft drink, the next he was standing there dead.

"It's hard to be dead," he told the chubby, greasy cashier.

Even so, he didn't disembody when he died, in the restaurant or anywhere else, so he probably wasn't dead now. Maybe he's dreaming then. It's a possibility. Well, it's not an impossibility, that's for sure. Is it?

It is. He's had the same dream every night of his life and in the dream he always wakes up standing on the ground staring at a wall, not laying on the ceiling staring at his body. He is twenty-eight years old as of yesterday and has had this dream approximately 9,855 times—he started remembering it on his first birthday, when, coincidentally, he uttered his first word: "Pterodactyl!"—and to all of a sudden have this other dream, for no reason whatsoever, was more than a little improbable. Considering that he did and thought the same things yesterday as he did and thought all of the yesterdays prior to yesterday, his unconscious routine had no motive for representing (or rather, for misrepresenting) his conscious routine in a way that differed, however slightly, from the usual way. That's what he told himself anyhow. Then he told himself: So if I'm not dreaming, I must be awake, in my body, looking at my reflection in the ceiling mirror. There is a mirror on the ceiling, isn't there? That would explain the chilly sensation on my back. Or would it? Because if I was looking at my reflection in the ceiling mirror I wouldn't be laying on the ceiling, I'd be laying on my bed, a waterbed with a heater cranked up to the max, meaning my back shouldn't be chilly, it should be warm, too warm. My back should be on fire!

And so it was. His back *was* on fire, and the fire was so hot that his back was chilly, so chilly. All he needed to do was reach over the side of the bed and turn the heating console down. Then there would be nothing left to concern him, nothing at all, and he could go back to sleep.

"Unless," he whispered, "the heating console has see-through lips . . ."

THE EQUATION

Professor Pedagogue paces up and down the aisles of the lecture hall, breathing vulgarities. He's trying to remember the equation. Trying—and failing.

A giant suitcase full of chicken sandwiches lay wide open on the main floor of the lecture hall. The professor was kind enough to bring them into class today. So far, none of his students has made an effort to stand and approach the suitcase to get a sandwich, worried they might bump into the professor and be assimilated. Everybody that has ever physically touched him has been assimilated into his persistently naked flesh and a handful or two of students suspect that Professor Pedagogue, who doesn't make a habit of bringing chicken salad sandwiches into class, has brought them in today for the sole purpose of prompting them to stand and approach the suitcase and along the way bump into him so that he may assimilate them. The sandwiches, in other words, might be the bait. Then again, the professor is more or less a decent human being and cares about the welfare of his students; he has no reason to absorb and kill them.

If he doesn't remember the equation, however, a reason may present itself . . .

Professor Pedagogue is prone to temper tantrums, especially when he can't remember things, a disturbingly routine occurrence, and if in the next minute he fails to remember the equation he will start flinging his body onto his students, screaming and crying and sucking one after another into his hungry pores until he does remember the equation, at which point he will cease playing the impetuous murderer and write the equation down on the blackboard with a piece of shrieking neon chalk . . .

A minute passes. A full minute, and his memory has yet to speak! Incensed, Professor Pedagogue flings himself on one, two, three, four students. There are over 100 students attending his seminar today and each time one of them is murdered those that remain gulp in terrified harmony, save Student Sarcophagus, who is asleep and snoring like a sea creature. The professor doesn't notice his lack of consciousness. He's too caught up in murder and in his defective mnemonic faculties to notice it, and when he reaches out to touch him with a finger—despite the professor's unrelenting rage, he's so old and grey he can't fling his body on more than four students in a row without getting all cramped up; but touching them with a finger produces the same effect as touching them with his entire body—it is entirely by chance. But just as his fingertip is about to connect with the tip of Student Sarcophagus's nose and vacuum the nose and everything attached to it into oblivion . . . his memory breaks its silence.

(Oblivious to his near death experience, Student Sarcophagus goes on sleeping and snoring. Probably for the best. Should he wake up, he's bound to regurgitate one or more of the small animals his pledge trainer forced him to eat last night during the orgy at the Chi Omega sorority house that his fraternity attended.)

Professor Pedagogue hurries over to the blackboard and begins scribbling down the equation. The equation is long and complicated, full of symbols the students have never seen before (some of the symbols don't even exist), and as he scribbles he encourages the students to come get a sandwich. "I worked hard on those things last night," he says. "Plenty there for everybody. And if you're really hungry, I have another suitcase full of pickles and potato chips out in the trunk of my car. Just let me know." Even though this verbal gesture is mistaken by a number of students as an indirect apology for the four murders he committed—the professor would just assume retire before apologize for assimilating a student, which, as a professor with a certain talent, not to mention tenure, is his right—still, nobody makes a move for the sandwiches: the book smart students are madly copying the equation into their notes, the common sense students are screwing wine corks into their ear holes to filter out the shriek of the professor's furious chalk. (Student Sarcophagus, who has neither book smarts nor common sense, has been devoured from the inside out by a black squirrel that now sits in his seat like a giant, hairy tea bag, dead from overindulgence.

Ed Screwtape, head janitor of Pseudofolliculitis State University, flows into the classroom, sweeps the squirrel into a big dust pan with a broom and disappears through a trap door in the spacetime continuum.)

"Right," says Professor Pedagogue, turning to the class and slapping chalk dust from his palms. "Now who wants to take a stab at this? Student Chromatic? Student Haberdasher? Student Vonk? No? Perhaps a sandwich might elicit a little garrulousness in you. Here you go." The professor removes three sandwiches from the suitcase and one by one whips them at their targets. Student Chromatic deflects the sandwich with a beat up copy of *Gravity's Rainbow*. Student Haberdasher ducks. Student Vonk ducks, too, but not quickly enough, and the sandwich strikes and explodes on her forehead. Chicken salad drips into her eyes and down her face and as she wipes it off Professor Pedagogue picks up another sandwich and stuffs the whole thing in his mouth. He swallows it in one gulp. He burps with pleasure, and raises and eyebrow. His students stare at their laps. "None of you people have anything to say about the equation? Nobody can explain this to me?" Silence. So Professor Pedagogue, after inventing and unleashing a barrage of obscene neologisms, explains the equation himself . . . to himself, in si-

- 204 -

lence. The book smart students take notes on the silence. Then the professor's silence breaks and he goes off on a tangent, and they take notes on that.

The tangent, which Professor Pedagogue speaks aloud, is about going off on tangents. It evolves into an elaborate lecture on tangents that involve the discussion of tangents about going off on tangents. Midway through the lecture a foghorn can be heard blowing in the distance. The students begin packing up their things. Some are already packed up and get out of their seats to leave.

"Sit down or die," says the professor. "I still have a good ten minutes left before I'm through with my tangent, and then, of course, we have to revert back to the equation. I understand that some of you may have other classes to attend. But that can't be helped, no, that can't be helped."

Grumbling, the students stop packing up and those that have stood sit back down . . . except for Student Protégé, who makes a break for the nearest exit door. Usually he would never think of acting so defiantly, especially when a professor like Professor Pedagogue gives him an order. But he had an exam in Professor Praxis's class in an hour and needed the time to do a little cramming.

"You! Protégé!" shouts Professor Pedagogue and immediately begins chasing him up the aisle. "Stop this instant or I'll shoot!" By shoot Student Protégé knows that the professor means he will throw himself at and assimilate him, but the professor will have to move fast at this point because now the student is just a few seconds away from being through the exit doors and out of range.

"I'm sorry, sir!" huffs Student Protégé, glancing over his shoulder. "I'm really sorry but I hafta go!" This plea, however, does little to appease Professor Pedagogue: despite shin splints and shot knees, he accelerates.

"Protegé! I say, Protegé! Don't be a fool! I'm telling you, I don't want to do it to you, so don't you do it to me!"

Student Protegé has a better than average student-teacher relationship with Professor Pedagogue. He respects him, and the last thing he would want to do is disappoint or offend him. But in this case he has no choice: unless he passes Professor Praxis's exam, he's going to fail the class and lose all of his student loans. Then again, if he doesn't obey Professor Pedagogue and stay put, there's a chance he's going to die. Either way it's a risk. The question is: Which risk is riskier?

In the same instant that Student Protegé asks himself this question he answers it, deciding it would be better to die than to lose his school loans, in which case his college career would be over. He lunges for the exit door as if it might be the ribbon of a finish line . . . but the door, unfortunately, has been locked from the outside by one of Professor Pedagogue's faithful TAs (Teaching Androids), and he crumples into it like a piece of tinfoil. A moment later Professor Pedagogue has pounced on him.

"Forgive me," the professor whispers as Student Protegé vanishes into his flesh with a slurp. Then he gets to his feet and brushes himself off. Without a word, he strides back down to the main floor of the lecture hall, sighing and shaking his head. He feels very badly about assimilating Student Protegé. Usually he feels nothing when he assimilates his students, assimilation is just part of the routine, something that happens when he loses his temper or is trying to make an important point, and while his students of course try to avoid assimilation if they can, they understand, accept and submit to its inevitability. But Student Protegé was special. Not only was he one of the only students to attend Professor Pedagogue's office hours, his motive for doing so was not, like the few others that attended, rooted in ass kissing. So the professor gives the student a short eulogy before returning back to his tangent, and then, at last, back to the equation. The eulogy is in the form of an epithet. It is read by Professor Pedagogue in a deep-seated baritone that, Student Orlick remarks to Student Ashenbach when class is finally let out for the day, is reminiscent of the voice of Professor Pejorative, Pseudofolliculitis State University's poet laureate.

> Full fathom five
> Student Protegé lies
> In my belly
> In my body
> His flight from me—not wise, not wise
> But tomorrow is another day.

IN SUPERCALIFRAGILISTIC CITY

In Supercalifragilistic City a man hides in the depths of a lynch mob. The lynch mob is stringing up everything and everyone in its path—butchers, UPS couriers, salesmen, mimes, hookers, stray cats, fire hydrants, etc. swing and twitch overhead like a swinging, twitching jetstream—but soon the mob runs out of materials, so they quickly string up themselves, exposing the hiding man—to Supercalifragilistic City.

In Supercalifragilistic City excuses are illegal. In Supercalifragilistic City happy hour is every hour and everybody makes barn yard noises when the bar tender's back is turned, hoping to drive the bar tender insane. In Supercalifragilistic City one may be either anorexic as a praying mantis or obese as an oinkhog: there is no in between.

In Supercalifragilistic City the mode of currency is ear lobes. Back when this mode was inculcated, the denizens of Supercalifragilistic City willed their ear lobes, once hacked off, to grow back; and the rapidity of this regenerative process, which cannot be willed faster, and which varies from denizen to denizen, dictates who be poor and who buys Pierre Cardin.

In Supercalifragilistic City males sniff out their female counterparts like fruit flies: with their legs. Noses are slopped up and down their legs like a bad case of poison ivy itching for that ineffable sex scent.

Dopplegängers on every street corner in Supercalifragilistic City hogging all the lampposts in Supercalifragilistic City.

Here is a poseur with a dirty word sheared into each of his eyebrows wearing fog-colored elephant leg pants and a knifenippled brassiere on the outside of his cashmere sweater vest. His toes have recently been stomped on by a stranger's heel. Was the stranger born in Supercalifragilistic City? If so, does he live on Kwazi Street? If not, was he born in Lagos, Nigeria? Do the streets in Lagos, Nigeria look like the streets in Supercalifragilistic City?

In Supercalifragilistic City there are no guns. There are Kafka-breathing sock puppets . . .

In Supercalifragilistic City everybody's first name is an adverb ending in -ly. In Supercalifragilistic City everybody wears name tags with these adverbs scribbled on them in neon ink. If you do not have a neon exclamation point at the end of the name on your name tag, in Supercalifragilistic City the penalty is an immediate cessation of chocolate rations.

In Supercalifragilistic City they brush their teeth ten times a day. In Supercalifragilistic City they grieve when a baby is born, rejoice when somebody dies. In Supercalifragilistic City they goose one another every chance they get. In Supercalifragilistic City they walk around with their flies wide open on purpose. In Supercalifragilistic City they go back and forth between the library and the movie theater all day long. In Supercalifragilistic City they realize the Lacanian real is a possible, tangible thing. In Supercalifragilistic City they double over with purple-faced laughter every time they fart out loud.

Inside the 747 that is passing over Supercalifragilistic City the pilots abandon the cockpit and start a food fight with the passangers and the passengers pelt them to death with goldfish crackers and finger sandwiches as the plane nosedives into the Abyss, a suburb of Supercalifragilistic City.

In Supercalifragilistic City scenes of bull-snorting pigeons, freeze-frame hubbly bubbly smokers and zoot suit blurs, pastiche of Chinatowns overlapping and cut-and-pasted together and stacked one atop the other like totem poles, orange swaths of cloud tearing across the sky in fast-time all the time in the shape of shape-shifting jack-o-lanterns, a Jesus Freak vomiting in a manhole, sound of a cash register, a car horn, an electric banjo, a conversation in polyglot, a dip spitball splatting against the ferroconcrete, monkchant sirens of the Dream Police, actors with identity crises sitting on café patios stuffing their screwed-up faces with key lime pie, rollercoasters full of screaming grand-mothers threading through Supercalifragilistic City in an end-less spider web of adrenaline, a thousand bald-headed Foucault clones in mirrorshades inciting loiterers of no consequence to riot out the corners of their ersatz mouths, a thousand gigantic vid-billboards on which Big Brother dressed up like Neil Dia-mond (dressed up like Elvis) sings the refrain of *Solitary Man* with a drunken out-of-tune slur while at the same time a thou-sand Venus fly traps perched on window sills snap out the beat to Queen's *We Will Rock You* . . .

The first half of the name Supercalifragilistic City, the out-of-towner might be surprised to discover, is not a clipped, slightly altered version of Mary Poppins' feelgood, game-play-ing word supercalifrajalisticexpialidocious. Rather, Supercalifragilistic is a portmanteau word encompassing the words supernumerary, caliginous, fragmented, ill-natured and ballistic—all words, not coincidentally, that might be used to describe the character of the handlebar-mustached Founder of Supercalifragilistic City, who built this place with his bare hands out of nothing more than a pissoir.

In Supercalifragilistic City I once saw the Founder lean over to kiss a baby in a stroller and instead of kissing the baby he bit off its head and spit it in a spittoon he keeps inside his over-coat. (Of course, everybody, including myself, cheered and broke out into song.)

In Supercalifragilistic City the graffiti on the walls is sen-tient and shits rabbit pellets in your eye sockets if you look at it too close, too hard.

In Supercalifragilistic City there are only two doors. Hanging over the front door of Supercalifragilistic City is a sign that reads: WELCOME TO SUPERCALIFRAGILISTIC CITY!!! Hanging over the back door of Supercalifragilistic City is a sign that reads: WHERE DO YOU THINK YOU'RE GOING?

ERASERHEAD PRESS BOOKS
www.eraserheadpress.com

Eraserhead Press is a collective publishing organization with a mission to create a new genre for "bizarre" literature. A genre that brings together the neo-surrealists, the post-postmodernists, the literary punks, the magical realists, the masters of grotesque fantasy, the bastards of offbeat horror, and all other rebels of the written word. Together, these authors fight to tear down convention, explode from the underground, and create a new era in alternative literature. All the elements that make independent films "cult" films are displayed twice as wildly in this fiction series. Eraserhead Press strives to be your major source for bizarre/cult fiction.

SOME THINGS ARE BETTER LEFT UNPLUGGED
by Vincent W. Sakowski.

A post-modern fantasy filled with anti-heroes and anti-climaxes. An allegorical tale, the story satirizes many of our everyday obsessions, including: the pursuit of wealth and materialism;the thirst for empty spectacles and violence; and climbing whatever social, political, or economical ladder is before us. Join the man and his Nemesis, the obese tabby, and a host of others for a nightmare roller coaster ride from realm to realm, microcosm to microcosm: The Carnival, The Fray, The Garden of Earthly Delights, and The Court of The Crimson Ey'd King. Pretentious gobbledygook or an unparalleled anti-epic of the surreal and absurd? Read on and find out.

ISBN: 0-9713572-2-6, 156 pages, electronic: $4.95, paperback: $9.95

SZMONHFU
by Hertzan Chimera

Fear the machine - it is changing. The change comes not only from the manner of my life but from the manner of my death. I will die four deaths; the death of the flesh; the death of the soul; the death of myth; the death of reason and all of those deaths will contain the seed of resurrection. This is the time of the stomach. This is the time when we expand as a single cell expands. The flesh grows but the psyche does not grow. That is life.

ISBN: 0-9713572-4-2, 284 pages, electronic $4.95, paperback $15.95

THE KAFKA EFFEKT
by D. Harlan Wilson

A collection of forty-four short stories loosely written in the vein of Franz Kafka, with more than a pinch of William S. Burroughs sprinkled on top. A manic depressive has a baby's bottom grafted onto his face; a hermaphrodite impregnates itself and gives birth to twins; a gaggle of professors find themselves trapped in a port-a-john and struggle to liberate their minds from the prison of reason—these are just a few of the precarious situations that the characters herein are forced to confront. *The Kafka Effekt* is a postmodern scream. Absurd, intelligent, funny and scatological, Wilson turns reality inside out and exposes it as a grotesque, nightmarish machine that is always-already processing the human subject, who struggles to break free from the machine, but who at the same time revels in its subjugation.
ISBN: 0-9713572-1-8, 216 pages, electronic: $4.95, paperback: $13.95

SATAN BURGER
by Carlton Mellick III

A collage of absurd philosophies and dark surrealism, written and directed by Carlton Mellick III, starring a colorful cast of squatter punks on a journey to find their place in a world that doesn't want them anymore. Featuring: a city overrun with peoples from other dimensions, a narrator who sees his body from a third-person perspective, a man whose flesh is dead but his body parts are alive and running amok, an overweight messiah, the personal life of the Grim Reaper, lots of classy sex and violence, and a fast food restaurant owned by the devil himself. 2001, Approx. 236 min., Color, Hi-Fi Stereo, Rated R.
ISBN: 0-9713572-3-4, 236 pages, electronic: $4.95, paperback: $14.95

SHALL WE GATHER AT THE GARDEN?
by Kevin L. Donihe

"It illuminates. It demonizes. It pulls the strings of the puppets controlling the strangest of passion plays within a corporate structure. Everyone, every thing is a target of Mr. Donihe's wit and off-kilter worldview . . . There are shades of Philip K. Dick's wonderfully inventive *The Divine Invasion* (minus the lurid pop singer), trading up Zen Buddhism for unconscious Gnosticism. Malachi manifests where Elijah would stand revealed; and the Roald Dahl-like midgets hold the pink laser beam shining into our hero's mind. Religion is lambasted under the scrutiny of Corporate money-crunchers, and nothing is what it seems." - From the introduction by Jeffrey A. Stadt
ISBN: 0-9713572-5-0, 244 pages, electronic: $4.95, paperback: $14.95

SKIMMING THE GUMBO NUCLEAR
by M.F. Korn
A grand epic wasteland of surreal pandemic plague. Pollution quotient in the southern delta nether regions of the state of Louisiana, the dustbin of the Mississippi river and the nation, whose motto is the "Sportsman's Paradise" but is a paradise of colorful denizens all grappling for a slice of lassez bon temps roule, "let the good times roll", but now all are grappling for their very lives. Nature had to fight back sooner or later, and now what will happen to this tourist state gone amuck with middle-ages plague?
ISBN: 0-9713572-6-9, 292 pages, electronic: $4.95, paperback: $16.95

STRANGEWOOD TALES
edited by Jack Fisher
This anthology is a cure for bland formulaic horror fiction that plagues supermarkets and drugstores. It shames so-called "cutting-edge" publishers who are really just commercial wannabes in disguise. And opens doors to readers who are sick of writers afraid to break out of the mold and do something/anything different. Featuring twenty insane tales that break all rules, push all boundaries. They can only be described as surreal, experimental, postmodern, absurd, avant-garde or perhaps just plain bizarre. Welcome to the dawning of a new era in dark literature. Its birthplace is called STRANGEWOOD. Featuring work by: Kurt Newton, Jeffrey Thomas, Richard Gavin, Charles Anders, Brady Allen, DF Lewis, Carlton Mellick III, Scott Thomas, GW Thomas, Carol MacAllister, Jeff Vandermeer, Monica J. O'Rourke. Gene Michael Higney, Scott Milder, Andy Miller, Forrest Aguirre, Jack Fisher, Eleanor Terese Lohse, Shane Ryan Staley, and Mark McLaughlin.
ISBN: 0-9713572-0-X, 176 pages, electronic: $4.95, paperback: $10.95

COMING SOON:
"Skin Prayer" by Doug Rice, "My Dream Date (Rape) with Kathy Acker" by Michael Hemmingson, and a reprinting of "Electric Jesus Corpse" by Carlton Mellick III

Order these books online at **www.eraserheadpress.com**
or send cash, check, or money order to 16455 E Fairlynn Dr. Fountain Hills, AZ 85268

CHAPBOOKS

Georgie and Her Meat by Joi Brozek $2.50
House of the Rising Sun by Gene O'Neill $2.50
From the Bowels of Birch Street by Kevin L. Donihe $2.50
Ballad of a Slow Poisoner by Andrew Goldfarb $2.50
The Baby Jesus Butt Plug by Carlton Mellick III $2.50
A View from the Shelf by Vincent Collazo $2.50
The Less Fashionable Side of the Galaxy by M. F. Korn, D. F. Lewis, and
Hertzan Chimera (collaborative stories) $2.50
The Hack Chronicles by Vincent W. Sakowski $3.00
Dancing Skinless (anthology) erotic surrealism $3.00
Knock the Dead (anthology) zombie stories $3.00
The Infant Vending Machine by Carlton Mellick III $2.50
Reconfiguring Frankenstein by Jeffrey Little $2.50
The Earwig Flesh Factory #3/4 (anthology) $3.00
I Gave at the Orifice by Mark McLaughlin $2.50
Neurone Fry-up by Hertzan Chimera $2.50
Kafka-Breathing Sock Puppets by D. Harlan Wilson $2.50
Wet Dreams of the Pope by Bart Plantenga and Black Sifichi $3.50
Sick Days by Shane Ryan Staley $3.00
This Year for Christmas by Wiley Wiggins $2.50
The Earwig Flesh Factory #2 (anthology) dark surrealism $3.00
Results of a Preliminary Investigation of Electrochemical Properties of
Some Organic Matrices by David Kopaska-Merkel (*Bram Stoker Award
Nominee*) $2.50
Much Ado About Teeth by Food Fortunata $4.00
Sycophantic Peepshow by Jon Hodges $2.50
The Adventures of You and Me by Aidan Baker $1.50
The Earwig Flesh Factory #1 (anthology) dark surrealism $3.00

Coming Soon:
Uncle River, Simon Logan, Paul Bradshaw, Everette Belle, Eve Rings,
Mark Blickley, Carlton Mellick III, and Vincent Collazo.

For shipping and handling, please include $1 for one book, $2 for two
books, or $3 for three or more books. Purchase chapbooks online at
www.eraserheadpress.com or send cash, check, or money order to 16455
E Fairlynn Dr. Fountain Hills, AZ 85268

Printed in the United States
3953